# Notes from the Nineties
## Stories and Poems

M Thomas Apple

KINOSHITA KAJITSU
New York / Kyoto

Portions of "Cois Fharraige" were previously published in *Scholastic Magazine* (Feb 27, 1997), vol. 138, no. 14.
"Ag an gCrosaire" and "Grandmother" previously appeared in *The Juggler* (1997).

Excerpts from W. B. Yeats, "Cuchulain's fight with the sea" from Ovid, "Metamorphoses," 4, 565 ff, printed in accordance with fair use of materials in the public domain.

Proofreading by Kara Lewis and Melodie Cook.

Author website: http://mthomasapple.com
Facebook: http://facebook.com/mthomasapple
Twitter: https://twitter.com/manzano0627

ISBN-13 978-4-905426-67-7
ISBN-10 490542677

# Table of contents

## Stories                                       *poems*

## September to April

*September*

I want to do a creative graduate thesis, he said.
In that case, you should keep a diary, his advisor
suggested. Write every day.
OK, he said.
And bring me a story or two to look at.
OK.

*October*

These aren't stories, his advisor informed. These are more
like diary entries.
How should I write a story, then? he asked.
Write what you know. Base your stories on people and
things around you.
OK.
And bring me another story or two.
OK.

*November*

The narration isn't believable, his advisor imparted.
Why? he asked.
It's too difficult for the reader to identify with the
characters. Nobody has a family with nine children.
What should I do?
Go read Sherwood Anderson's *Winesburg, Ohio*.
OK.

And bring me a couple more stories.
OK.

*December*

I don't get any sense of through-story, his advisor
complained.
What do you mean? he asked.
The stories aren't connected. They're all different.
Well, what should I do?
Try an internal perspective. Go read James Joyce's *Portrait
of the Artist as a Young Man*.
OK.
And bring me another story.
OK.

*January*

This is too abstract, his advisor mused.
What do you mean? he asked.
This isn't a true plot. The symbolism is too obscure.
It's a translation of something I wrote for a German class.
You don't want to be Kafka.
I don't?
You need real life stories, with real people and real
problems.
What should I do?
Go read Raymond Carver's "Cathedral."
OK.
And…
Bring you another story?
Two.

*February*

I think I see the problem, his advisor intuited.
What is it? he asked.
I think you need to experience more life before you can be an effective writer.
What do you mean?
You need to go out into the world and work different jobs, meet different people, move around a bit.
My thesis is due in two months.
So it is. Make sure you give your draft to me next month.
OK.
And...
Another story?
No. Just read my comments and rewrite what you have.
OK.

*March*

I don't see the point of adding poetry between the stories, his advisor grumped.
Why? he pondered.
The poems interfere with the prose.
I thought you didn't like the prose.
I would say you need to add a poetic sense to your prose.
How do I do that?
Try writing poetry. For practice.
...
And finish the rewrite of the draft by next week.
OK.
And print three copies on a laser printer. And buy three of those thesis black cover binders.
OK.

*April*

Well, the three of us have examined your thesis, and we decided on a grade of B+, his advisor beamed.

…

I know it's not as high as you wanted, but I argued that the interplay of letters, poetry, and stories woven together formed an interesting kind of metadiscoursal narrative depth to the thesis structure.

…

Congratulations.
Thanks.

# Cois Fharraige

*Cuchulain stirred,*
*Stared on the horses of the sea, and heard*
*The cars of battles and his own name cried:*
*And fought with the invulnerable tide.*

All told, it took them two hours deciding how much alcohol to buy for their Conamara beach party. Tom had sat at the wooden table outside the local pub "An Cistin," downing pints of Irish heaven while the others from his summer language school debated how best to divvy up their much-depleted funds. The American male contingent had decided that they ought to get some whiskey but couldn't seem to decide how to proceed from there, as Ray had already bought himself a little bottle, and Nathan himself had been enjoying a pint or two. The two Norwegian women, Suzanne and Sara, and Annie, the woman from Chicago, had already bought some wine, but Annie agreed with her fellow Americans that whiskey seemed a good idea as well. Andy, a black-leather clad native of Seattle with the habit of spouting well-worn Black Adder and Monty Python phrases, stood somewhat apart from the group, silently smoking and watching the world through unnecessary sunglasses. Marin, her arms crossed, talked quietly to him in a crisp London accent, occasionally pausing to tap her thin glasses into place with a delicate hand. Stefan, the towering bearded Bavarian with curious oval glasses, didn't care what kind of alcohol they all brought to the beach, so long as the women were there.

In the end, Nathan headed off to the liquor store, and the others began to consider walking. They delayed sufficiently until Andy decided it would be a good idea to return to his house for a torch. The group now numbering about a half dozen, they tossed back their pints, pulled their jackets tighter and finally set off to the beach. As he lifted the plastic bag containing the four cans of draft Guinness worth ten pound (according to the bar master), Tom looked after the slender figure of Marin in her pink turtleneck shirt. He thought he saw her up the road to Andy's host house, but whether going or coming, he couldn't tell. Reluctantly Tom left her behind and quickened his pace to catch up to the group ahead on the darkening horizon.

Twilight had come to Cois Fharraige. The sea breeze into the village of An Cheathrú Rua had begun to pick up a bit, but it was still relatively warm out for July in the west of Ireland. The group attracted a few more random students from the six-week Irish language program, here one from Michigan, there another from Australia, as the narrow road was winding them past small modern houses, buffeted by stone walls to the left and right. They passed two high schools, one on each side, and large chaotic groups of young teenagers swept by around them, heading the opposite direction, singing the chorus of the Cranberries' song "Salvation." The pupils stopped, each calling out to the older foreign students in high-pitched sharp Dublin accents, practicing summer Irish: "Dia dhuit, dia dhaoibh. Hello, hello."

About halfway there, just before the turn from macadam to dirt and gravel, Tom looked over his shoulder and spied three figures in the distance, following on the road. Nathan, Andy and Marin, he surmised, turning his attentions to the road itself. Large patches of animal dung appeared underfoot, splotched across the tarmac as the group made a left turn near the top of a hill. Tall grasses bordered the ubiquitous stone walls, interrupted only by closed iron gates in front of a few houses, some abandoned long ago. Once in a while a gnarled, stunted tree stood guard over a newly-graveled driveway, but otherwise there were few trees to be found across the dull brown-green landscape.

After another twenty minutes of walking, Tom could no longer distinguish the stone walls from the cut peat turf neatly stacked on rocky barrens behind them. The bay appeared over the horizon stretching from left to right out into the endless Atlantic, light rapidly failing as they slowed their brisk pace. The end of the road opened out into a tiny, empty car park, three white stone slabs to the right leading downward to a long concrete ledge bordering the back of the beach area. Behind the ledge, on a slight incline to the right of the stairs, spread a grass-overgrown cemetery.

They had been to Cemetery Beach before, Tom remembered, during one late afternoon as the rays beat down on a rare sunny day. The beach was one of a half dozen on this particular peninsula of An Cheathrú Rua, looking out across a small inlet at the one-story white houses which dotted the grey- and green-mottled hills. At nighttime now the tide was in, stranding in six feet of water the far end of the line of the small boulders which marked the beach boundary. It was as the group was sitting down and collectively sighing after the hour-long walk that Tom asked, "Where's Nathan with the whiskey?"

He was nowhere to be seen, though had he been standing ten feet from the beach, no one would have known. "He'll be along," Annie said, "I think I saw him back aways." She opened her backpack and extracted two bottles. "Here's some wine, if you want some," she said, offering one of them to the group.

"Thanks, that's okay," Tom said. He popped one of the Guinness cans he had brought, resting it on the coarse sand as he waited for the foam to subside. Ray brushed back the corners of his moustache with a forefinger and thumb, shaking his head. He pulled out the hip flask from his denim jacket and proceeded to congratulate his foresight.

"I hope that Nathan der Weise has not dropped the bottle of whiskey somewhere in the dark," said Stefan, pronouncing his 'th's as slight 'z's. He stood, hands in his pockets, and began to dig a trench with his boots. Tom took another swig from his canned stout, watching the lights across the bay flicker on one at a time. The sea breeze seemed to pick up, the night growing visibly darker. His companions seemed no more than dim silhouettes along the shore, red tips of cigarettes dancing in the air. At last someone said, "Maybe we should make that fire now."

Annie's cigarette bobbed. "Yeah, it's getting colder."

Diligently Stefan continued his work. Tom pulled out a newspaper from his bag and tossed it in Stefan's direction. "I'd be willing to go look for some wood," he said, "except for the fact that I can't see a damn thing."

"Here," said Annie. She tossed him a small torch. "Don't lose it."

"Yeah, okay." Tom turned towards the car park. A bouncing beam of light announced Andy's appearance, as he strode down the road bellowing in his stage voice, "Here I come to save the day!" Marin quietly followed, slowly curling wispy blond hair around a finger and smiling. Carrying a brown grocery bag close behind was Nathan. "Hey, everybody, anybody want some chips?"

"Hey, Andy," Tom called out, walking towards the newcomers.

"You mean crisps?" Marin asked with a smile, darting a look at Andy before heading toward the main group.

"It's Underdog! TA da dum ta da da DUM! Hey, what's up Tom?" Andy asked, swinging his torch around and pointing it at random objects, holding one hand against his waist and puffing his chest out comically.

"Uh, yeah, right," Nathan replied. "Here, would you like to open a bag?"

"We can use the newspaper for starter, but we need wood for the fire, so I thought we could look over here near the rocks for driftwood," Tom said, flicking on the mini-torch with his thumb.

Andy paused and cocked an eyebrow. "Why, that's a good idea, a very good idea indeed. You take this side and I'll go over there."

"Hey, be careful, guys," Nathan called back as Andy and Tom started clambering around the mossy rocks. "You might twist an ankle or something."

Andy turned his torso and shined the light directly upon Nathan's face. "Don't worry, citizen," he said with a tight-lipped confident nod. "We're experts at this sort of thing." Nathan and Marin disappeared into the dark, where Tom assumed from tiny red lights and slowly rising conversation the group still to be.

The two picked among the debris for a few minutes, finding not much of anything worth burning. Tom eventually shook his head. "Andy, this is all I could find," he called out, holding up a handful of twigs in that direction. A beam of light struck him in the eyes as Andy replied from a short distance, "Okay, I think I'm going to go a bit further."

"Andy," Tom said, trying to block out the light, "I can't see anything."

"Oh," came the reply, moving away. "Sorry about that."

Tom headed back to the beach and ran into Stefan, who was returning from the road and dragging a small tree branch behind him. "Hey," said Tom, "I didn't know you had gone looking for wood."

"I didn't," Stefan chuckled, his laugh sounding a bit like a hyena and a tad high-pitched for a two-meter tall man. "I went up the road to relieve myself behind a wall and I tripped on this." He shook the branch. "There are too many leaves, but..." He shrugged.

Tom nodded. "Well, I didn't find much," he said, "so I guess we'll take what we can get." Stefan dropped the branch next to one of the Norwegian women, Suzanne, who was rolling up the newspaper into balls and tossing them into the makeshift fire pit. She got up briefly to grab a lighter from one of the smokers, and Tom tried arranging his bundle of twigs in a teepee shape. "This is going to be the world's smallest campfire if we can't find any more wood," he said as Suzanne silently lit the newspaper in two or three places. Andy arrived and added some fuel to the fire. He stood back a couple of steps and lit a cigarette, staring into the young flames.

Tom remembered he still had a Guinness in one hand and tilted it again. He sniffed the air to his right. "Hey, Andy," he asked, "are you still smoking those cloves?"

"Hmm?" said Andy, taking the cigarette out of his mouth. "Oh, yeah, of course." He replaced it, grinning. "I love 'em. And nobody asks you for a cigarette unless they're really desperate." He turned back to the fire and continued smoking.

Tom finished his can and walked around the fire to rest his back against the ledge. An unopened bag of potato crisps lay in the sand at Marin's feet. Hands folded in her lap, she looked up as Tom sat down heavily. "Cé'n chaoi a bhfuil tú?" she greeted him.

"Réasúnta...go maith," he said, dropping the empty can into his bag. "And how have you been?"

She smiled and nodded. "Tá mé go maith freisin." She looked at the fire, then back. "Cé'n chaoi a rinné tú ar do scrúdu?"

Tom paused. "How did I do on my test? I dunno, I screwed it up, I think." He lowered his head, unsure what next to say, then looked up to see Andy towering over him. "I'm going up to check out some of the gravestones," he said, motioning with his torch, "so if you need to, you know, do your duty and whatnot, I'll be up there with this.

"Oh, and before I forget," he added, "if you spot my lighter, would you grab it for me? I don't want somebody walking off with it." He straightened and grinned. "You know...sentimental value."

Marin watched him go and bit her lip, returning her gaze to the fire. The gathering had increased in volume with the addition of at least a half dozen more people. Walking back in forth in front of the fire, Annie sang the chorus from "Killing Me Softly" a few times and tried transposing it into Irish but failed to move any of her listeners into joining her. She stopped to refresh her voice.

"Hey, how about an Irish song?" Nathan asked from his prone position further down the ledge.

Annie lowered her bottle and looked startled. "What, me?"

"No," Nathan said, "I mean anybody. What about those songs Mícheál taught us yesterday in class?"

"Hey," Tom said suddenly. "Where's that whiskey at?"

"Over here," Nathan said, waving the bottle.

Tom lurched to his feet and grabbed it. "Already half empty? Jesus." He took a few swigs from the bottle and gave it back. Nathan and Annie debated for a few minutes who was to sing, before Annie wandered into another conversation and Nathan hit the bottle again. Feeling slightly hazy, Tom ambled across the sand to the boulder boundary, maybe ten or fifteen meters from the fire but still within earshot. The conversations' pitch assumed a curiously rhythmic mixture of relaxed murmuring and riotous laughing. "Andy?" Tom called, peering up the brick wall. "Hey, Andy, you here?"

"Yo." Andy thrust his torch light over the wall and down at Tom. "Hey, c'mon up here and check out some of these gravestones."

"Hang on, I gotta take a leak."

"Sure." The beam of light wavered as Andy switched his grip and angled the torch to Tom's left. "You might want to go over there behind the rocks somewhat, I mean, if you like your privacy and all."

"I can't see where I'm going."

"There you go."

"Okay, thanks." Tom unzipped his fly and the light was withdrawn. Sensing the pints he had earlier in the pub were finally hitting home, Tom concentrated on a patch of moss at the bottom of a rectangular rock at least at tall as himself. He finished and, looking up, spied a set of large white steps five or six meters to his left. Carefully maneuvering between the rocks, he ascended the steps, turned to his right, and found himself on top of a grave. The waist-high weeds parted as he tried to find a path between the graves. Ahead he saw Andy's light and made his way towards it. Andy was crouched on another weed-covered grave, shining his torch at a weathered stone and mouthing the barely legible words.

"Oh, hey, Tom," he said, not turning his head. "Check this out."

Tom bent and squinted. "What's it say?"

"Looks like Mary O'...something... born eighteen eighty-something, died nineteen oh six."

"So it's in English?"

"Yeah, most of the ones I've looked at are. Kinda disappointing, but, y'know, if I found any in Irish I wouldn't be able to read them anyway." He moved to the next stone and scraped away some of the moss.

Tom hesitated, then moved himself to a neighboring site. "I don't know," he said, "what if this is, like, a family grave plot or something?"

Andy shook his head. "I doubt it. Families would keep their graves cleared. I don't think anybody's been back here in years."

Tom looked down. "There's flowers on this one."

"Really? Cool." The light shone on a square stone set flush in the ground. A bundle of decaying flowers lay beside the stone. "Well," ventured Tom, "I guess the flowers have been here awhile, but somebody must have been here pretty recently, at any rate."

"Huh. What's the stone say?"

Tom read: "Máiréad Ní Fhlaharta, 1925."

"That's it," he said, straightening. "No age or anything. Must have been just a baby."

"Yeah, that's kinda sad." Andy let the light rest on the stone for a moment.

"Hey, Andy," Tom said, "this is changing the subject, but you know Marin?" He put his arms parallel in front of him, hands bent at the wrist, and made a panting noise.

Andy grinned. "Sorry. I don't get your meaning."

"Puppy dog. She's following you around like a puppy dog, man."

"Really? I hadn't noticed." Andy arched an eyebrow. "Gee, I'm sorry, man. I mean, if you have designs on her..."

"No, nothing. Sure, I guess I'm jealous, but, I mean, how long are we going to be here? Another week?" Tom put his hands in his jeans pockets and glanced back to the campfire crowd. "What could happen?"

"Yeah, you're right." Andy stood and turned off the light, speaking in a conspiratorial tone. "She told me she's already got a boyfriend back in England, you know."

"Yeah?"

"Yeah. Like, they've been living together four years or something. So I don't know what's going on. It's weird."

"I get the feeling everyone here is just out for kicks, you know, some of them are married, like Stefan. It's like they just don't care."

"Yeah, well, I dunno." Andy clicked on the torch again. "You going back?"

"Yeah, I'm starting to feel thirsty again."

Andy nodded and grinned. "Okay, think I'm going to stick around here for a while."

"Okay. See you." Andy plunged farther into the underbrush, and Tom took a few awkward steps before stumbling onto another set of steps leading back to the concrete ledge. He stepped over outstretched legs in front of the fire and picked up a warm can of Guinness from his bag before plunking himself down next to Marin. She made no response, simply gazing blankly into the fire and holding her hands in front of her. Tom stared into the purple-blue flames along the sand.

15

Three bricks of peat fell on top of the fire from Sara's outstretched arms, sending a few sparks into the air. She stooped and stacked a few random twigs and leaves on top of the bricks, her short auburn hair dancing in the sudden flickering illumination.

"Where did you get the peat?" someone said.

Sara looked around with a blank expression. "I found them along the side of the road." She continued putting twigs on the fire.

Tom set down his can. "You mean you just took them from some guy's back yard?"

"There were plenty of them there," she said. "They won't miss a few." She added the remainder of the small quarrel on top of the peat and walked toward Stefan, who was standing, hands still in pockets, talking to the drinking men down the ledge.

At Tom's right, Marin stirred. "I don't think she should have done that." Her lips made a slight noise as she spoke, a moistened sound at the beginning and close of the sentence.

"No," Tom said quietly.

She spoke again. "I don't like that."

"Neither do I," Tom said. They both fell silent as the conversations around the fire rose and fell in pitch like waves, occasional ripples of laughter rising to the top and rapidly descending. A few people left. The flames became dark orange again as the bricks finally caught, the leaves sending puffs of smoke skyward. The peat would burn, Tom knew, but it would not radiate much heat. Tom stretched his toes out; even from a distance of a foot, he could not feel any warmth. He dropped the empty can and opened a third.

Holiday, a holiday, first one of the year
Lord Donald's wife come to the church
the gospel for to hear...

Tom stood at the sound to his right. Stefan was standing, swinging the whiskey bottle to a phantom beat. Sara and Suzanne were sitting in front of him on the ledge next to the almost still forms of Nathan and Ray. The two women urged Stefan to continue. Awkwardly, he stopped, and held out his left hand with fingers curled and twitching. "I should have brought my guitar," he giggled drunkenly. "It sounds much better with guitar."

"Go on," mumbled Nathan from his prone position on the ledge. He waved a limp arm in no particular direction. "Don't need guitar."

Stefan sang haltingly.

She cast her eyes about
there she saw little Matty Groves
a-standing in the crowd...

"No," he said, shaking his head. "Ní cuimhin liom...I don't remember all of the words."

Tom rose from the sand. "Come home with me..." he supplied, taking a drink from his Guinness,

Come home with me, little Matty Groves,
come home with me this night
come home with me little Matty Groves
and stay with me till light.

"Ah," said Stefan, taking over:

Oh I can't come home, I won't come home,
I can't come home this night,
By the rings on your fingers I can see
you are Lord Donald's wife.

And what if I am Lord Donald's wife,
Lord Donald is not home,
he's out in the far away fields
bringing the yearlings home.

Tom extended a hand for the whiskey bottle, but let it drop when he saw it was empty.

But a servant standing by heard the news,
took to his heels and ran
I may be my Lady's servant,
but I am Lord Donald's man.

Stefan's voice quavered as if he were uncertain of the lines. Tom opened his mouth, but decided not to tell Stefan that he had dropped a verse, instead covering his momentary pause with a drink from the can. Quickly Stefan's hands jumped into a guitar pose and he mumbled, "Da Da, da da dum da dum, something like that." He continued, his voice gaining strength:

So then she took little Matty home
and it was there they fell asleep.
And when he awoke the very next day
there Lord Donald was at his feet, saying,

And how do you like my featherbed,
and how do you like my sheets?

And how do you like my lady fair
who lies in your arms asleep?

And it's well that I like your featherbed,
and it's well that I like your sheets,
but it's best that I like your lady fair
who lies in my arms asleep.

The words disappeared into the night like a whisper.
Stefan stopped, and began to mumble again, "Scheiße,
was ist das nächste...Ah!"

Get up, get up, little Matty Groves,
get up quick as you can,
for never it be said in fair England
I slew a naked man.

"Fair Scotland," Tom said.
"Ireland, Scotland, it all depends on where you are,"
Stefan said, shrugging.

I can't get up, I won't get up
I can't get up for my life,
for you have got two beaten swords
and I have got a knife.

It's true I have got two beaten swords,
they cost me dear in the purse,
but you shall have the best of them
and I shall have the worst.

Tom joined in briefly at that point. Stefan didn't seem
to mind, the two singing not quite in harmony:

And you shall strike the very first blow
and strike it like a man,
and I shall the very next blow,
and I'll kill you if I can.

And Matty struck the very first blow,
hurt Lord Donald sore.
Lord Donald struck the very next blow
and Matty struck no more.

Tom dropped out again. Stefan continued in an almost monotone, rocking back onto his heels and chanting the words as fast as possible:

And up he caught his own dear wife,
and he set her on his knee, saying,
Who do you like the better now,
little Matty Groves or me?

And up spoke his own dear wife
never heard to speak so free,
Better a kiss from dead Matty's lips
than all of this finery.

And up Lord Donald did jump,
loudly he did bawl,
pierced his wife right through the heart,
pinned her against the wall.

And a grave, a grave, Lord Donald cried,
put these lovers in.
But bury my lady at the top,

she was of noble kin.

Again Stefan's hands came to life and he attempted to mimic the closing riff, concluding with a "dum DUM!" A few people clapped and he took a short bow before depositing himself to the sand. Stefan sighed. "I know of two versions of that," he muttered, "maybe three, but I can never remember all the words." Tom remained standing alone before fire. Already it seemed on the verge of extinction again.

By the time he returned to his original seat, the group had lessened its number by half. Annie had finally convinced a few people to sing eighties' refrains with her. They still stood down near the water, smoking in a circle, shivering and singing out of harmony to "Roxanne." Ray was gone, having needed three to carry him up the road.

Tom sat rooted in the sand, his back to the ledge, staring into the flames. A few more minutes and they would be dead and gone. The peat was crumbled into ashes, unrecognizable. He thought he had seen Stefan and Sara a short while ago. Sara, sitting on the ledge, and Stefan standing in front of her. Tom picked up the last can.

"Later, Tom." Andy. Leaning forward, shaking hands, confidentially. "I've got an appointment to break. Tell you tomorrow." Wink, nudge. Marin left with him.

"Oíche mhaith. Ee-uh wah. Good night, ladies. Goodnight ladies. Good night. Goodnight."

Tom held the can in his right hand. The left slowly plucked the tab forward and back. A hiss, and the brown foam gurgled out. The breeze picked up again, blowing the smoke up from the firepit. All over his hand. Smoke swirled in strands, silver glitters upward into the dark.

Twirling down his wrist. Tom closed his eyes and felt tiny ashes touch his face, his palms. Dripped onto the sand.

## Ag an gCrosaire

As I sit here stranded
on this moss-covered rock letting the wind
scrape my thoughts through mire's
flesh-covered bone

I feel my
self down through the knees
through the stone for the home that
was not, nor is, nor ever
could be.

O Érin, as Éirinn,
what have you to offer me:
a few bitter roots, restless rotting tubers
of the past, history-forgotten reminisces
of what it meant to have
a soul.

When the only sounds left me
are the ticking of my heart,
the curtainy ocean mists,
the loving whisper of the colleen of Oisin,
what else can you tell me here
that I do not already know.

## Father Knows Least

My father is a nerd.

It just struck me the other day at the end of the winter break. You know, I always wanted the perfect Dad, the one that all my friends seemed to have, the dad who would hand you twenty bucks and the car keys and say, "Have fun, now" as you peeled out of the driveway in his Trans Am. I always wanted a father who didn't treat you like a baby and didn't act like such a schmuck.

I always wanted a father like that.

"Don't you feed these boys?" the Coach once asked my father at high school Open House (a misnomer if ever there was one). Half joking, half serious, all insulting.

Standing outside the locker room and P.E. office, I had wanted to raise my hand to answer. Like I was at Sunday School, answering a question from Sister Bea.

"Daniel and his brothers lived on bread and water, so can I," I'd say proudly. Puff out my scrawny chest.

Or, "Actually, no, we're kept locked up in the cellar, running the treadmill to power the hot water tank for the bath." Yeah, that'd go down.

My father blinked. "What?"

Fathers on the whole tend to blink, I think. It makes them appear mildly aloof and covers up the fact that they simply aren't paying attention much of the time. Or maybe they're just too busy figuring out their next "old man" one-liner.

My dad has always had this annoying habit of cracking bad jokes and then laughing at them. And he never passes up the opportunity to embarrass me in front of my friends.

Whenever my high school teammate Thad called, saying "Is John there?" Dad'd say, "Well, mostly." Ha ha. Funny, Dad.

When some girl would call, "Can I talk to John?" he was always, "Well, sure, you can. Oh, sorry, I thought you were taking a survey."

Yeah, that must have been the reason. Great. Girls like Dweeb Dads.

And every time we'd go out to work in the backyard garden, he found it so hilarious to make a joke out of the garden hoe.

"Hoe, hoe, hoe, Merry Christmas. Hyuk, hyuk."

Whatever, Dad. Funny.

My brother Craig and I would roll our eyes or just look at each other with contemptuous smirks, and I knew we were both thinking the same thing:

"What a dork."

That's another thing. My father has this bizarre concept of "dirty language." Whenever Craig and I said certain words, like "dork" or "hell" or whatever, Dad'd frown and squint at us over the rim of his glasses.

"Stop using foul language."

OK, so "dork" technically means "penis." Big freakin' deal. It's just an expression.

My father gets even madder when we say "suck."

"The Mets suck again this year."

"They stink. They do not suck. Vacuum cleaners suck. In most countries, 'suck' is a bad word."

"They suck. Boy, do they suck. They sssuuuuhhhhh-uck."

Arguments are frequent around my house, I've noticed, compared to my college friends'.

And then there was that time I was still in high school when we rented "Ghostbusters," which my Dad had never seen before. Do you remember that scene in city hall, when Ray explains that the ghosts had escaped because "dickless here opened the containment unit" — "dickless" being some policeman or somebody standing in front of Ray. I forget who it was exactly, some guy.

At any rate, the Mayor turns to this guy and says, "Is this true?" And Bill Murray pipes up and says, "Yes, your honor. This man has no dick."

So we all laugh our asses off, all of us except Mr. Morality, who just sits there on the living room couch crossing his arms, frowning and sticking out his bottom lip at the TV.

"Only stupid people swear."

"Huh?"

"People swear when their vocabulary is so limited that they can't properly express themselves, so they resort to vulgarity instead."

"Oh, Larry," my Mom butts in. "You're so full of shit it's coming out your ears."

"You say such nice things around your kids. Why don't you just add to the hatred and aggression a little more?"

"Up yours. Just because your parents were prissy and coddled you, you spoiled little baby…"

"That's it, go on the attack! Try to make it a confrontation! That's what you're so good at! Why don't you…"

"…bastard, son of a…"

"…just keep it up in front of a five-year-old, do you think…"

"…fuck you and all your fucking kids! You can sleep on the couch, you're not getting any tonight…"

"…you're such a good example of a loving mother…"

"…just fuck off!"

"Fine!"

And then Mom flips him the bird and stomps upstairs and slams the door behind her. Dad slouches in the couch and squishes his face together, like he wants to say something nasty but can't do it. Craig and Luke and the rest of us just stare blankly at the movie the whole time, pretending not to hear them. It was always like that, Mom shouting and slamming doors and Dad whining and then shutting up with crossed arms. No idea why they stayed together. Must have been us kids. And little Ben wasn't even born back then.

I think maybe that's why at some point my Dad gave up trying to convince me and Craig to stop "swearing." He tried stuff like, "Everything you do is imitated by your sister, Lisa, so watch what you say and do."

"She's twelve. She can do whatever the hell she wants."

"Not in my house she can't! And watch your mouth, mister."

I just wished he'd give it a rest already. I mean, it's not like we go around saying "fuck" after every other word like those junked-out drop-out zombies who hang around the school playground. They're just pathetic. And he did give up, at some point. I don't remember exactly when. Maybe right around last June when we got into the finals and I blew that last game.

See, I somehow managed to get into college last fall. This past summer, after I graduated. I couldn't get a baseball scholarship but I managed to get a couple small local awards and a Pell Grant and borrowed the rest. Dad co-signed, of course. Still held on to my part-time gig at Mickey D's down the road here about three, four miles, so when I visited between semesters for the winter break I could still make a few bucks cleaning the deep fat fryer. Minimum wage, of course, $3.35 an hour, same as the last three years. No raises for people who don't work at least six months straight, the manager told me. What bullshit.

Yeah, so when I came back, my room was gone. The room was there, I mean, but the bed was somebody else's. It's funny, sleeping on the couch and getting woke up every morning by tromping little feet running to the Bran Flakes table. Christmas was like it's always been, three to four hours of non-stop unwrapping and Elvis Presley and

Bing Crosby Christmas songs on LP. I swear, my parents never stopped living in the '50s.

But it was what happened after Christmas and New Year's were over that was the interesting part. College break kept going another couple weeks, but Craig and Lisa and Brian and the others had to go back to school. That's how I got to finally experience a typical day in the life of my mother.

Ben's only a year and something and he just figured out how to walk, sort of. That means he's dangerous. He can even talk a little bit if you've been around him long enough, but if he doesn't know you, he'll just look cute and then toddle away. I've only been working every other day about four to five hours at a time, which is how they make sure you can't get lunch breaks or over time pay. So of course at home I had to watch Ben. It was easy at first; just turn on the TV and make him watch stupid kiddy shows on PBS. Problem is that I had to watch the same shows, so I started playing games with him instead. After a couple days, though, he really started getting on my nerves, so I tried to pass him off on Mom instead. She didn't like that and tried to ignore the both of us. Just sat at the dining room table and read trashy novels, eating "Dutch" sugar cookies and drinking tea. Man, she drinks tea. I swear, she goes through twenty cups between ten in the morning and two in the p.m.

Mom does have a lot of laundry to do. At least four loads of laundry every morning. In the summer she must hang it all up outside on the line in back, but in winter it snows too much, so the constant noise from the washer and dryer in the pantry room are just ear-splitting. But after that, she doesn't really do much. Except curse. She curses the news, curses Ben when he cries, curses at the dogs, curses at Dad when he's not there, curses at each individual family member except me. I figure she gets me when I'm at college, because, why not. She must swear because she likes it. Why else would she? I mean, sure, I swear sometimes. "Fuck this, the hell with that," whatever, whenever I got mad, in the locker room, on the team bus or out with the guys.

But my mother's made it a profession. I swear, she thinks it's her personal responsibility to criticize everything and everyone, like she thinks by calling my Dad a "fucking idiot" that he'll be able to suddenly buy a brand-new Silverado the next day. The crazy thing is my Mom insists that she loves me. She's already told me four times this break that while I'm at college in Albany she listens to tapes of me playing in high school band. And cries. Cries! It's not like I was any good at trumpet. I was too busy trying to make the starting rotation. But we never took any videos of my games, so I guess the tapes are all she's got.

So, what does she think when she's listening to my old high school band bleating? "That's my baby! I remember when I used to wipe shit from that bum of yours!" And then she smiles, like it's some wonderful secret that she wiped my ass when I wasn't old enough to even stand up. Get real. They say that daughters grow up to be like their mothers. I feel sorry for my sister's future husband in, what, ten years or something.

Speaking of Lisa, that real interesting part I already mentioned is about her. Her and my mother. This was yesterday around 7 p.m. I'd just opened the door, coming home from a rare double morning-afternoon shift that gave me a dinner break for the first time, like, ever, when I was assaulted by my Mom. Well, I guess assaulted is too strong a word, but it fits, the way she just throws stuff at you, like it's all your fault and you should do something about it right away or you'll be damned to hell for all eternity.

Lisa was all hunched over on the couch, holding her head in her lap, arms covering her face, bawling with her red hair all over the place. I guessed she was crying, anyway, since her shoulders were shaking and no noise was coming out.

"Your sister's a druggie."

My mother stood over Lisa, arms crossed in triumph, as if she were proud to catch her doing something "bad." I hadn't even taken my cap off, my mom launches into this story right in front of Lisa. Just to make sure my sister felt extra guilty and wanted special forgiveness for her venial sins. It took me a while to figure out all the details, because upstairs I heard my Dad and brother Craig shouting something at each other at the same time I'm trying to listen to this.

So I guess what's happened is that Lisa's been sneaking out of the house at night during the break. I'm talking she's leaving the house well after midnight and coming back around 4 or 5. She must have managed to sneak out a bunch of times without waking me up, which didn't surprise me. I always tell people an H-bomb could drop on the bar next door, and I wouldn't wake up. Which makes no sense when you stop to think about it, because I'd be dead. But it does in a way, because I sure wouldn't be waking up again.

Anyways, Lisa was going to the construction site for the new high school. Figures they'd wait until after I graduated to make a new school. Since it's the second week of January the workers set up huge heaters to get the concrete to dry and then put blue tarps over the heaters to keep the snow off. Lisa and three of her junior high friends were going there under the tarp for a "smoke." Dunno what it was they were smoking, but weed, I guess. My buddies used to do 'ludes but guess that's all over with now. I'm not saying whether I did either or not, but I sure wouldn't be dumb enough to do it at a school, even one still under construction. Two of Lisa's friends must have smoked too much and got sick, so they went to the hospital. Health center, I mean, then hospital.

My parents found out when the mother of one of the kids called our house this morning to spread the bad news. It had to be Lisa's fault, because her daughter would never do something like that on her own and so on. All when I was busy at work scraping off grills and squirting "special sauce" on burgers. After telling me the whole story, my mother just smiled. An evil, malicious kind of smile, the kind that doesn't quite reach your eyes. And said, "Your father's upstairs." I had kind of guessed that already from the noise.

It suddenly went all quiet up there. Then Craig came stomping downstairs, stuck his head in the living room doorway and glared at us, then yanked the front door open and left with a slam.

I shoved my hands in my pockets and yawned. This, I didn't need. What I needed was a good long shower. My black and orange work uniform still smelled of deep fry. I headed slowly up the staircase, the faded green steps creaking. Dad was in the bathroom at the top of the stairs, slouched in the dark, on the closed toilet seat with the mirrored medicine cabinet above him. As he turned in my direction, glasses off, I could see his face was gaunt, his beard looked whiter. Drained.

He tried to talk a few times but nothing came out. He turned his back to me, didn't even bother to hide the fact he had been crying. Eventually he spoke.

"I've tried to raise my kids the right way," he started. "I've always tried to do the right thing. I've made sacrifices for my family. I moved us to a bigger house in a better neighborhood. I got a better job. I put all my money into my family."

He was almost choking the words out, still not looking at me.

"Everything I do gets thrown back in my face. Your mother stabs me in the back every chance she gets. Nothing I do is good enough for her, and she's always rubbing it in. Craig takes adrenaline pills to beat up a bully at school, and when I call up the father of the kid who gives him the pills, I get accused of calling the kid a pusher. And in return Craig swears at the dinner table, runs upstairs and locks himself in his room, shouts curses at me the whole way, shouts how much he hates me and wishes I would die. And now, Lisa..."

He began to sob.

I didn't know what to say. I wanted to say something. Something like, It's OK, everything's fine. But it wasn't true. I wanted to say, You're always over-reacting. Knock it off. But I couldn't. For some reason, I just found myself placing my right hand on my father's left shoulder, and saying, "Dad..." And then stopping, swallowing, looking down.

He looked at me and said nothing. We stayed like that, my hand on his shoulder, for a couple moments. My father broke the quiet by rubbing his knuckles into his eyes, then his palms down his face and beard to his chest, smoothing out imaginary wrinkles in his shirt and straightening his tie. I dropped the hand. "Got to get back to the monthly budget," he mumbled, taking his brown plastic-frame glasses out of his shirt pocket and shoving them back onto his face as he stood. "I'm going to have to cut into the house heating oil fund to make the mortgage payment. Why don't you help your mother clear the dinner table?"

"Yeah, sure," I said, ambled downstairs, hands in my pockets again like nothing had happened. I took off my cap finally and threw it on a chair, then scooped up some stuff from the dining table. Mom was in the kitchen, putting a couple dirty plates into the dishwasher, without rinsing them first, of course.

"Did you talk to your father?" she called out, as if she were concerned, as if it were my fault.

"Yeah," I said, going over to put the milk back in the fridge. Thankfully, she let the topic drop and didn't speak again as we cleared the rest of the table.

Later that same night, the family—minus Craig and Lisa—gathered around the couch and said "prayers." Every night since I was a little kid, my family has said the Our Father and Hail Mary before going to bed. I don't really say them any more, so I just sit there with my hands folded and watch them pray. My mother set the tempo, talking very loudly and very slowly as she held Ben's hands together and tried to teach him the words. Ben just looked blank. Luke and Brian closed their eyes tight and prayed in loud voices, following my mom. My father didn't say anything. He just sat on the far end of the couch, folded his hands with his elbows on his knees and held his forehead in the space between his thumbs and index fingers. Lisa stayed in her room, crying loud enough for the six of us to hear downstairs. Craig hadn't come back.

After prayers, everyone said goodnight to everyone else, and my mom carried Ben up to tuck him in. Dad still sat there. Praying, I guess. Eventually he got up, said goodnight to me, and slowly walked through the front hall doorway, like he was carrying something really heavy. I think I heard him sigh, or maybe it was just the couch after he got off. I rolled out my sleeping bag on the couch, turned the dimmer light off, and went to sleep.

Today's been pretty much a normal weekend day so far. My father got a chance to live up to his hallowed title of Doofus on the Block by leaning his forearms on his snow shovel and yakking it up with the new next-door neighbor all morning while I shoveled the driveway myself. At some point Craig appeared from behind a snow bank, walked right past me, said, "Hey," and went inside. No mention of where he'd gone. I just nodded and kept shoveling. Probably a good work out for me, anyway, in the offseason. I don't blame my dad for not helping with the snow, what with his bad back and all.

Maybe he's OK, I don't know. He's still a nerd, like I said, but I guess he has a lot on his mind. Glad I'm not like my father. At least I get to go back to Albany in a couple days.

## Shinji-kun, No

Now the last night in my room
it is so strange
Another turning point — but every moment seems so

Every second a divulgence of possible paths
every path a future, all past

Walls look barren as they once were, stripped of all
pretenses
Shadows of posters checker-board the dull white
handprints in charcoal, all fingers and thumbs

Empty waiting for new ones to fill these pregnant spaces
soft pale under-middle easily torn away
casually excised and forgotten

        This place is gone
        though I am still here, tonight
        — This place is gone

I do not forgive
I do not forget
I expect what I demand, no more no less
I know jealousy beyond all bounds
—by imagining betrayed

She said perhaps we'll talk, I got bread and tea.
Perhaps.

No, you're not the One.

No, I'm not, either.

***Power    control    leech    drain    need
    desire        lacking***

***grace        integrity***
***                unworthy***

I cannot sleep I cannot eat I cannot think I was

Wrong to attach meaning
wrong to believe
wrong to read what I wanted
wrong to need
wrong for faith in anything in plans in you in me
wrong wrong wrong to care, too much

All is wasted all is none, I saved the worst for last,
even that now is fled.

All I have is Anger
to fill these empty shadows on the walls
Anger feeds as I feed it
will
make you regret this, will
make you reject me, will
make you regret this
taking of me.

Somewhere inside—a cry.

## The Firebrand

A twenty dollar bill becomes two fives and ten ones. Another twenty fills the gas tank and empties the wallet. And so the road trip begins.

The directions given me to the Bronx are clear: down the Thruway to the Major Deegan Expressway, take the second right, there's a little green sign, you can't miss it. Manhattan College, new home for my brother Craig, his first year at college. After Manhattan, we'll drive Jen to

JFK, where she'll board a flight to France for her year abroad. My father wanted to meet me and then go to the City together, but I thought it was easier this way. It's hot on I-90, upper nineties, in fact, but factory air-conditioning does the job. Cruising at 65, just a notch above the speed limit but a notch below everyone else, the Escort wagon remains relatively cool. The radio station stays static-free for about about an hour. Once that fades away, no amount of dial turning satisfies: oldies, pop, dance, all discarded with a flick of the wrist. Eventually the thin red line rests on all the same news, all the time. The window is rolled down further. Sunlight reflects from the dark blue hood, and a visor is flipped down.

Up ahead are five lines of cars. A sign can be seen. It reads, "Cars — $0.75." Waiting five or ten minutes, handing a bored man a dollar and getting a quarter, the car stutters forward, pretends to stall, then picks up the tempo again, following signs that go south. Up ahead is another one: Tappan Zee Bridge, $3.00 toll. The lines of cars extend for a mile. This wait is long. Rap blares from the ugly green Chevy in the next line. A hard rock station is quickly found, the radio turned up to compete.

Finally across the Tappan Zee, the traffic speeds up. There are four lanes now in each direction. Signs appear on each side of the highway, saying this parkway that way, this parkway another. Ignore the signs, continue southbound. Only fifteen minutes later steam rises from the front of the car. Cars are slowing. There aren't any accidents or delays or construction, what could the problem be? The inside of the car is getting hotter; the window is now rolled all the way down and an elbow is balanced on the edge for breathing room. A red Ford Festiva darts up the shoulder of the road. The hood is

39

shimmering now, the car sounds like a dragon. Something's wrong. It's nothing important, it can't be something important.

The highway splits beneath an overpass, two lanes form an off ramp, two lanes go slowly forward. The eighteen wheelers in the back begin to rev and snort. Time to pull over. With a disconcerting abruptness the car stops in the black top shoulder in the shade. The engine chatters and smoke rises from the cracks in the hood. Green drops fall from beneath. This is not good. The hood pops open and clouds of smoke billow outwards in one desperate gasp. Liquid bubbles in a plastic reservoir of antifreeze, boiling from underneath the cap. This is not good at all. I sweat.

A few more minutes and the bubbling stops. The antifreeze cap is still hot to the touch but can be opened easily. There is almost nothing inside — only a tiny pool left, barely enough to cover the bottom. It's good enough, it's got to be. Not much further to go, it will be good enough. The car jerks alive, draws a breath and limps back into the lane. It's getting hotter, the newsman says ninety-six. The car believes him. I hope my father appreciates this. A little green sign on a grey overpass says, "Major Deegan Expressway," another says, "233rd Street." Made it.

Okay, where's the turn? Where's the little green sign with my brother's name upon it? Signs for Fordham and Columbia, have I gone too far? There is a sign for the Triborough Bridge: that's not the right way, that's way too far. Face and neck are red from anxiety, or is that the heat? Look, there's the Cross Bronx Expressway — it stays in the Bronx, at least. Better than the Triborough. Turning left, now caught in transit, pushing, pushing too hard. 55, 60, 65; slow down, the car can't take it. The chattering gets louder. An overhead reads, "New England, left two lanes. Hutchinson River Parkway, right lane only." The engine protests as the wheel jerks towards the suicide seat. Cutting off a brown Dodge, shutting out a whining car horn, the car eases onto the gently curving ramp. Still going north, what do I do?

Another expressway ahead. Turn onto it, go west, back into the Bronx. The highway gives way to two lanes and a yellow center line. The dragon only grumbles now, but the window stays down, the radio turned up. The yellow line disappears, there are cars parked on both sides. Every hundred feet is a stoplight, and they are all red. A right turn puts the car on Fordham Avenue. The pavement is broken, bricks and dirt poke through the cracked slabs. There is a layer of haziness covering the road, blurring the air, distorting the clogged way. Cars and trucks are double-parked and triple-parked. Delivery vans stop in the middle of the road. Wavy images of men in stained light blue shirts jump down from the back, throw cardboard boxes to the sidewalk. Pedestrians and skaters dodge the boxes without looking up. Are these people crazy? The car swerves, jumps into where the opposing lane should be, then back, then out again, avoiding the bicyclists, the walkers, the open doors on parked cars. The city is a big pothole. The temperature rises.

I've got to get out of here. A left turn steers the car to a black iron fence surrounding a school of some kind. A passerby says to ask the security guard inside the gate, not her, and hurries away. The security guard, black, middle-aged, overweight, sunglassed, listening to the Yankees game on his walkie-talkie, grunts and shifts in his chair behind the fence. He says to turn around and go down Fordham, turn right here, left there, left again, you can't miss it, good luck. I thank him and turn around. He never lifts his head.

The car fears New York. It must be a hundred degrees, the street must be more. The wheel is painful to wrap a hand around. Leather bike gloves make it easier, trading one heat for another. Up Fordham, past expressway entrances, back the way I came. Through the obstacle course, around the skateboarders, underneath a railroad track, what is this place? The pavement is even again. Gas station to the right. The car lumbers into the lot and sputters as a man approaches. He glances at the hood. My cousin goes there, he says. Here's how you get there, it's pretty simple. Turn left, go back to Fordham, go for a ways, then see this sign and turn left again, you can't miss it. He is Italian and slaps me onna back. His watch says three p.m. — one hour late already.

The road smiles as the car returns. Following the instructed path, the car idles at twenty-five. A thrown switch vents heat into my lap, drawing air from the engine. The car is a firebrand, haze converges in front of the grill as we roll down the two, now four-lane road. The radio finds an FM station from Long Island University. It has advertisements and weather reports but claims to be pirate. Songs blare, but I don't hear. The car halts in a five-way intersection. There is another gas station with men leaning against the pumps, and I pull in.

The car door opens, and one of the men has already shaken his head. No speak English, he says. No speak English, no can help. He listens briefly, then changes his mind. 2-3-3, he says, 2-3-3, that way. He points up that way. No speak English. Two three three. The road finds me again, and there is another station to the left. There are three islands of concrete and a booth. Behind a glass window sits a dark thin man with a dark thin mustache. He speaks into a tiny microphone, Sorry, no English. Nothing else. His eyes look away, but he doesn't move.

There is a juice machine to the side of the booth. I have only a quarter, and it doesn't take dollar bills. The man in the booth doesn't give change. I turn back to the car with a raw throat. A young kid, maybe twelve but bigger than me, with a baseball cap and black tee-shirt, says he overheard. His mom can help. She's over there, by the pump. His family stays in the car, two older teenagers in the back seat stare out as the woman speaks. The older boy says, Yeah, listen to her, she knows where it is. The woman stares at the road, thinking. You lost in the Bronx? she says. Honey, you don't ever get lost in the Bronx. You won't get out. You stay on this road until the end. Don't turn anywhere, go to the end, it goes into Route 9. It's a few miles, but there's a big sign on 9. Just don't turn. I thank her. She nods.

Back in the driver's seat, I grip the wheel, rub my chin on my shirt shoulder. The radio says it is a hundred and three. Why didn't my father tell me it was on Route 9? My own college is on 9, my parent's home is on 9, my favorite beer store is on 9, and he didn't mention it? The car follows the nameless concrete, under bridges, past park, through light after light. A bank clock reads four. The family must be at the College by now. They must have left my brother the freshman at his room, hope they're still there with my sister. One last chance to see her for a whole year. The road curves right at its end, onto 9. The left lane is filled. I see a large green and white sign in a flowerbed: Manhattan College. The cars in front all have Manhattan decals and clothing obscuring the rear windshield. This must be the place.

The road now leads up a hill to a tall chain link fence. The car stops outside a brick security building. It wheezes and clanks for a while after the engine is turned off. The guards have guns and one tells me a room number, but he doesn't want to. He's my brother, I say. The guard writes down the number and the dorm and talks to the other, caressing his sidearm.

The car grinds to a start and back out onto the road. Another parking lot beckons ahead, behind a steel and glass sports arena, surrounded by more fences and tall red brick buildings, trees growing in perfectly hedged squares amongst them. The car pulls into the shadow of an oak tree and sighs. A walkway bridges the gap between the lot and the eighth story of a dorm. Blond ponytailed Manhattan sweatshirts seriously stride upon it. I find the sixth floor. There is a cleaning lady who says, This is not the right room, parents are staying here this weekend. They gave you the wrong room.

I leave her and find a map in the bottom floor lobby: I am in the wrong building. Craig's dorm is near the library. Walking over red and brown patios, small lawns with birch tree trunks wrapped in black metal bodices, my feet trudge to the dorm's door. The elevator is not working. I skirt the painter on the stairwell who mumbles in Spanish and reeks of cigarettes and alcohol.

I now notice my forearm and elbow, my forehead and face are bright pink and hurt when touched. I clutch the small piece of paper with the room number and enter a white hallway. A student, the Residential Advisor, sees me and asks if he can help. I say my brother's name, and he points to a door. He unlocks the door and leaves. I feel cool air, air-conditioning, from the other side. I turn the handle, push, and walk into a vacant room.

## I Obey the Law of the Hunt

I will Hunt again tonight I clean my instruments
meticulously, carefully prepare my sharpened barbs
I never return alone I am a good Hunter.

I clearly label myself my fellow Hunters will
not sight me I stalk with silence and diligence
I take careful aim I do not waste time or
munition. I am a good Hunter.

I do not hide I am clearly marked I am
dismayed sometimes but I never disappoint
I am calm I am patient I will always be
rewarded in the end. I am a good Hunter.

I do not understand why my prey does not
label itself like I I only wish to Hunt it
because it runs I wish to be efficient and
merciful I am labeled and it is not for it is
not me I wish it were easier. But I am a good Hunter.

I am labeled I do not hide I am clear
I stalk with pride I am calm I am a Hunter
I Hunt, that is what I do I know Death and
the Hunt. The Law needs no reasons.

# Kannuki

I was living in DC when I finally got the news. From a friend who'd moved out to the West Coast to be where things were happening. It was a shock, as all news are, when you get them too late to do anything, to change anything.

Bruce had died of "immune deficiency related complications" in Mercy Hospital. San Francisco. Do you think that was typical? ironic? par for the course. I don't know. The bastard. I wasn't in shock, no. Bastard.

My job remained somewhat hectic for two to three weeks after I received word of his death. I had to do something. In the end I had to tell my firm that I simply needed a day or two for personal reasons. I had been saving my sick days to add to my summer holiday, but these two days I knew I needed. Perhaps a sense of closure. Or melodrama. Or self-pity. Who could tell.

Jon took it stride. We'd both taken extended business trips, both been subject to that fear, or is it suspicion, that some business trips are more business than others. But we trusted each other. Without our trust, we'd never have lasted this long. I packed a light suitcase and spent the better part of an afternoon wrangling with a travel agency over plane ticket prices. Eventually something was worked out, and I transferred a couple times between DC and California, with lengthy stay-overs at each stop. I had brought some work from the office, since I knew there would be plenty of time on my hands. But I couldn't concentrate. There was too much time. Plenty of time to do nothing but think.

Standing at the side of a newly filled grave, I felt as if I had been traveling for ten days instead of ten hours. Maybe even ten months, or years. I think it had been at least ten years, though I'm not certain. A sudden panic had overtaken me at that spot, waiting in a cemetery on a cloudy day, clasping my hands in front of me, waiting for something to happen.

Nothing did, of course. I had come too late, too late for even the funeral, which was just as well, I supposed. I hadn't had to endure the sight of him, weakened and tired looking, seeming too old for his thirty-three year old body.

I hadn't the chance to sit at the side of Bruce's bed, holding his wizened hand, to try to smile weakly yet reassuringly as we both temporarily forgot exactly how much I detested him.

I wondered what I would have said to him, had I known in time. Assuming I would have made the visit in the first place. How many times is it that you have known friends or former acquaintances laid up ill, and yet chose not to make an appearance? How many times have thoughts such as these come back to haunt you, trouble your dreams, make you wish you hadn't been so ignoring, so cold, so...thoughtless. But then you do it anyway, without thinking. No, with lots of thinking. Too much.

I had closed my eyes, tried to imagine myself at Bruce's side. I could see his eyelids flutter as I walked in the door, feeling ill at ease, uncomfortable before a man I once thought I knew, and now could barely recognize even by physical appearance.

"Robin," he would croak, attempting to flash his old crooked, wicked grin at me.

"Bruce." I reply. "It's...good to see you." I sit in the wooden chair graciously provided by the nurse attendant. Reflexively I let my hand fall towards the bed, and Bruce weakly but firmly seizes it.

"It's been so long," he says faintly. Bruce pauses to cough into his fist, turning away briefly. He takes a deep breath, but his shallowing breathing is painfully obvious. "You...you're looking good, Robin."

I shake my head, glance over his bed to the television hanging from the ceiling, and then back to him. Bruce always knew I hated being called Robin. Feh. Robin Boy Wonder to his Bruce. Why should I expect he be any different, even on his deathbed.

48

"Look, Bruce, I..."

"You know," Bruce softly interrupts, squeezing my hand again and again, "I wasn't sure you would come. I'm...I'm glad you did." He smiles and tries to stroke my hand, rakes rough, dry skin against me, and falls back into his pillow, closes his eyes.

I attempt to clear my throat. I don't know what to say. I don't know if I could say it, if I did know. How to treat the man who ruined my young life?

"Are you with anyone?" Bruce suddenly asks, turning his head on the pillow.

Startled but not entirely surprised, I rapidly retract my hand. "Yes." I stopped and started again. "Yes, his name is Jon. We've been together nearly nine years now."

Bruce nods his head.

"He's...good to me, very good to me," I say haltingly. "We've been good for each other, I think."

From somewhere Bruce summons the strength to reach for my hand and hold it tightly. "I'm happy for you," he grins crookedly again.

I bow my head. I know I should feel pity for this man, grief, immense sadness. But I can't find it within me to feel sympathetic for him. Years ago, he never cared. Before we saw each other, while and after we saw each other, Bruce was one of the most sexually active...abusive...people I knew. He screwed everything that moved...well, on two legs, at any rate. If there were others, I didn't want to know.

I wasn't exactly prudish myself. I'd always felt a bit regretful about what had happened during my brief period of studying in Japan, but whatever I had done, Bruce had outdone me. After our short and extremely eventful stay together, he'd left in the middle of the day when I was working, taking all the cash he could find, without leaving a note. Two days later he had called me from Chicago, acted as if nothing had happened, and hung up when I began to break down on the phone.

Later that month I received a postcard, stamped from San Francisco, giving the address of a mutual acquaintance. He made it quite obvious why he was staying there. I never wrote.

At the gravesite, I could still imagine seeing him there, lying in the hospital I never visited, trying to act as if we had no history. Nothing in the world would have mattered to him but that moment, nothing in the world would have mattered but him, to him.

And now back home I can still see me standing there at his grave, wondering if he had been remorseful, wondering if any of our old friends had been to the funeral or even visited him in hospital. Wondering if things could have possibly been any different, or if I could have felt any more empty, or powerless. Wondering when he got it, how long he'd had it, and where I was along the way.

Wondering if we were really no different, in the end.

Damn him.

Parallel Conundrum

These things do not matter:

        Every day becomes the first and last,
the people all come and go,
all blend into one long empty memory
of me.

        These people — you,
you are a ghost the day after tomorrow;
you will become yet another image my mind
creates in its spare time

                envisioning

your
smile, creating new words to replace the
old, new feelings and meanings you needed but
body language to express.

                I will

manufacture a perfect likeness of you,
and it will never leave,
and it will not grow old or stained,
and it does not need you or me,
in my dreams.

        You are already dead to me,
      and life couldn't be better.

## Boys Will be Boys

Jayson was nine when his family moved away from his relatives to a small town upstate. It was a strange feeling for him, having his own yard, not having cars in the street out front, not hearing noises at night. There were no children his age within miles of the house, and he quickly became tired of playing with his two younger brothers.

There was only so much he could do inside a chain-link fence.

One day in early July, a week or two after the end of the school year, Jayson's father asked him if he wanted to visit his grandparents and uncle at their summer camp for an overnight stay.

"Grandma and Grandpa said they'd love to have you," Father said. "You can stay there for a week, if you'd like."

Jayson was pleased. He asked, "Will Uncle Lennie be there?" Uncle Leonard was three years his elder, the older brother he never had. Jayson idolized his Uncle. He would have done anything to impress Uncle Lennie, anything to gain his favor. Anything.

Father nodded.

Jayson beamed. "When can I go?"

He arrived at the summer camp in the morning. The camp was founded and run by the family's Methodist Church, but hardly anybody seemed to use it. His grandparents always camped there every summer in a tiny fold-out trailer and stayed at the same spot, nestled between two rows of tall blue spruce trees next to a wide softball field. The trailer was surrounded by a clothesline of giant beach towels, forever in the shade. Jayson and his uncle had to sleep on the trailer's inside kitchen table, which could be lowered between the folded-out side compartments and made into a bed. On his first day at the camp, he and Uncle Lennie played frisbee and went swimming in the small man-made lake the campground bordered. It was hot.

One of Uncle Lennie's friends visited the next day. He and Uncle Lennie went to the big softball field to play catch. Jayson asked if he could join. "I brought my baseball glove with me!" he said excitedly. "It's in the trailer."

Uncle Lennie smiled. "Sure. We'll wait for you right here."

Jayson ran back to the trailer. He looked anxiously for the glove for a few moments, but couldn't find it anywhere. He trudged back to the field. "Gee, that's too bad," said Uncle Lennie, as he threw an orange softball to his friend. "If I had an extra one, I'd let you use it, but I don't. Sorry."

Dejected, Jayson slowly walked to the edge of the field and sat on a huge rock to watch his uncle and his uncle's friend throw the ball back and forth. When it got towards dark, after Uncle Lennie's friend had gone home, Jayson thought he heard funny squeaking noises all around. Then he saw a dark cloud emerge from over the treeline with the red sun behind it. "Wow!" he shouted, standing up. "What's that?"

Uncle Lennie walked over to the boy. "Bats. They only come out at night, 'cause they're blind."

"Are they vampire bats?"

"Well," Uncle Lennie smirked, "some of 'em eat bugs, but some of 'em like to suck blood, too, 'specially the blood of little kids like you."

The boy looked sideways at his uncle. "You're making that up."

"Oh, no," Uncle Lennie protested, "I'm not lying, I swear." He swiped an index finger over his heart twice to make a cross. "But I think we'll be safe in the trailer, as long as we keep the windows closed."

"Okay," Jayson nodded, watching the growing cloud spread into the sky above them. He shuddered, then composed himself as they returned to the campsite.

Uncle Lennie's friend stopped by to visit again the following day. The three of them, Uncle Lennie, his friend, and Jayson, went down to the lake to go fishing. Jayson brought the rusted brown tackle box that he had borrowed from his father. At the dock, he took out a small glass jar and grabbed a worm out of the wet shredded paper inside. Uncle Lennie's friend laughed at him.

"Hey, you should use this," he said, pulling out an open package of hotdogs from a brown paper bag. "Them fishies, they don't want worms. Would you wanna eat a slimy worm?"

Jayson looked at the worm, then back at the friend. "Yuck," he said, and threw the worm into the water. The friend tore off a piece of hotdog and put it on the hook on Jayson's fishing line. "Go on," he urged, with a smile. "Go to the end of the dock. That's where all the fish are."

As Jayson walked down the wooden planks, he heard the friend whisper, "Does he know how to swim?"

"Don't," Uncle Lennie said. "My mom'd kill me."

Jayson awkwardly cast the line out and watched the red and white bobber hit the water surface. He waited. After a while, he reeled the line back in, then felt water trickling down the back of his shirt. He turned around and saw the friend aiming a small yellow squirt gun at Uncle Lennie.

"Hey, don't look at me," the friend said, smiling.

Uncle Lennie and his friend laughed.

Jayson bit his lip and cast the line out again. As soon as the bobber hit the water, the line jerked downwards. Jayson strained to keep the pole in his hands as the bobber moved to the right. He pulled back and up and began to reel the line in, shouting, "I got one! I got one!"

Uncle Lennie was at his shoulder, holding his arms steady as he slowly cranked the reel. "I don't believe it," muttered the friend, as a foot-long pickerel slapped up the side of the dock's wooden pillar. Jayson grinned. "You were right! They do like hotdog!"

Uncle Lennie didn't say anything right away, as he took the hook out of the fish's gasping mouth. "You know," he started, "you can't keep him."

Jayson didn't understand. "What do you mean?"

"Well," the uncle said, looking at his friend, "it's not big enough to keep. It's got to be at least a foot and a half. This one's only a foot."

Jayson was downcast. He held the fish, stroking its prickly scales but avoiding the sharp fins. "Besides," the uncle continued, "you'd have to rip its guts out and chop its head off and stuff. Grandma won't do that for you."

Jayson sighed. "Okay," he said, and reached over the side of the dock with the fish.

"No!" shouted the friend. "Gimme."

The friend grabbed the fish, whipped it over his head, and flung it as far as he could out into the middle of the lake. Jayson watched his fish hit the water and send up a sudden splash just before it disappeared. The friend seemed pleased at himself. "Hey, hey, didja see that? Pretty good, huh?"

"Yeah, pretty good," Lennie replied.

The friend held the remaining part of the hotdog near his crotch and shoved the squirt gun into it. "Hey, watch this!" A small stream of water ejected from the tip of the hotdog. The friend swung the hotdog back and forth over the edge of the dock, spreading water around him. "It's my hotdog, look at my hotdog!"

Jayson closed the tackle box and fastened the metal clamps.

"Let's go," said Uncle Lennie. "It's getting dark."

On the third day, Uncle Lennie told his nephew that he would teach him a new game. "C'mon, Jay, let me make it up to you for the other day," Uncle Lennie said. "Follow me. I want to show you something." He gestured away from the campsite, further into the pine trees. Jayson hesitated, but only for a moment.

The two walked out of the trailer site, over a clay and moss-covered forest floor, emerging on an old, forgotten dirt road with two worn tire ruts and a tall grassy meridian. Only the chirruping of the eastern bluebirds and the June bugs, the crunching of fallen pine needles underfoot interrupted the walking silence. They passed out of sight of the trailer and the nearby softball field, moving deeper into the woods. Around a turn in the truck-wide path was a small clearing of stunted grass and white flowers. It was here that the uncle instructed his nephew to lie on his stomach with his pants pulled down.

Jayson didn't understand. "It's easy," Uncle Lennie said, demonstrating. He dropped his shorts past his knees. Jayson did the same and turned around to lie down. "No, you have to pull your underwear down, too." He did.

Jayson slowly lay down between the flowers on top of a moist slender green carpet. Uncle Lennie slowly lay down, his lanky form all but covering the smaller boy. The boy felt the increasing weight of his uncle, the cold sensation of flesh upon flesh. He rested his forehead on his arm and smelled the damp dirt. He watched a group of blank ants carry cut leaves underneath his nose as Uncle Lennie whispered into his ear over and over, "It's all right, I'm not going to hurt you. You know I'd never hurt you…"

After a few minutes, Uncle Lennie got up. "Okay, now it's your turn." The uncle took his place in the damp grass, his white briefs down around his ankles. "Go ahead. It feels good."

Jayson obeyed, without knowing why. He pulled out his penis and held it in his hand, laying on top of mountain of pink flesh, rubbing back and forth. He felt tiny. His breath came in short gulps and his forehead prickled from where it had rested upon his arm. "It's all right," Uncle Lennie repeated. "See? It feels good, doesn't it? Doesn't it?"

Later that night, by the campfire at the trailer site, his uncle grabbed him by the shoulder and pointed through a patch of small bushes to the next campsite over. "See that chick over there? Man, I'd like to slam her hard."

Jayson looked through the bushes and saw that there was another family camping there near a similar trailer. He saw a girl in a tight, pink one-piece swimsuit walking around a stone fireplace. He shrugged. "Why would you wanna do that for?"

Uncle Lennie stared at him. "'Cause she's a girl, dummy." Grinned and punched him in the shoulder. "What else do you think you do with girls?"

Jayson didn't say anything, so the uncle punched him again, harder. "Huh? Huh?" Another punch, and Jayson clumsily slapped back. The uncle moved, and Jayson's flailing arms made him stumble forward. He tried to recover, but Uncle Lennie was upon him before he had a chance, tackling him to the ground in front of the fireplace. The two laughed as they wrestled in front of the fire, casting dancing shadows against the trailer's aluminum side. The grandparents looked on from their lawn chairs, Grandma saying, "Isn't it good that the boys are getting along?"

Grandpa poked at the fire, snapping his dentures.

The rest of the week went by quickly. Jayson's father arrived after lunch on Sunday to pick him up. "How did the week go? Did you have fun?"

"Yeah!" Jayson enthused. "Me and Uncle Lennie, we did all kinds of stuff. We played frisbee and we fished, and we played softball."

"Sounds like you had a lot of fun with your uncle."

"Yeah, he even taught me a new game."

"A new game, huh?"

"Yeah, we got bored 'a the same old things. It's kinda different than the other games."

"Really? Tell me about it," Father said, interested.

"Um," Jayson paused. "I'm, uh, not sure that I should."

Father stopped. "Why?"

"I promised. I promised I wouldn't tell anybody."

Jayson looked down. Father put his hands on Jayson's shoulders and knelt in front of him with a serious expression on his face. "Jayson, tell me."

"Well, um. OK. First, uh, we went a ways away from the trailer, off in the woods someplace…"

"You went into the woods…" Father said slowly.

"Yeah. I lied down, and then he, uh, he, uh…" Jayson frowned. He didn't know how to explain. It was his uncle. Anything.

Father stood up slowly, his face red and contorted. He hands covered Jayson's shoulders, and he spoke through thin lips. "You stay right here, okay? I have to go talk to your uncle."

"Okay, Dad," Jayson said. He watched as Father entered the trailer. Jayson shrugged his shoulders and started throwing a tennis ball into the air and catching it. He heard someone shouting, then realized it was his father. After a moment or two, Uncle Lennie came out of the trailer and stood by the fireplace. Father followed. Father stood with his hands at his side as he talked to Uncle Lennie. Uncle Lennie crossed his arms and hung his head while Grandpa and Grandma appeared from inside the trailer. Grandma slowly walked over to Jayson, holding Jayson's two brown grocery bags full of clothes for the week. Grandpa's face was closed up tight as he stood next to the trailer door and stared into nothing. Grandma hugged Jayson and kissed his cheek. Grandpa just stood there, scratching his right forearm.

Leaving Uncle Lennie alone at the fireplace, Father walked over to Grandma and touched her shoulder. "Mom," he said, but didn't finish. Father took Jayson by the hand. "Say goodbye to Grandma and Grandpa," he said quietly. "We've got to go."

"Bye," the boy said obediently. "Thanks for letting me stay here, Grandma."

Grandma kissed his cheek again and patted him on the head. "You be a good boy, you hear?"

"I will," Jayson nodded. "Bye, Grandpa."

Grandpa grunted.

Jayson and his father walked out from under the pine trees and into the gravel parking lot where their maroon Chevy Nova waited. Jayson sighed. Back to boring home. Nothing to do except play with his dumb brothers. He put the two grocery bags into the back of the car and, to his surprise, saw his missing baseball glove at the bottom of one of them. Father started the car as the boy pulled out the glove and put it on. He briefly wondered when he would see his uncle again.

M Thomas Apple

## 1,000 Isles

Summers of my Upstate youth were spent
in the family station wagon, the six of us—
or was it seven—
traveling to the great St. Lawrence
Seaway of a thousand islands.

The first time, we stayed one night
—Mosquito Heaven,
sleepless in a brown canvas tent—
then four more nights on the biggest island,
half in the US,
half out.

I learned how to gut a fish, how to swim,
how to roll up a sleeping bag,
and where to buy fireworks—
I mean sparklers.

On my 12th birthday, I got a wallet,
put in a year's allowance,
then when I forgot it in the campsite bathroom,
got advice in return the next morning—
"I told you so."

Looking back, it makes sense
to me now
that I hate dressing.

## Grandmother

father there is a spider in my room

    whenever I am still
    for a while, she pokes her head out
    from a corner of the ceiling
    and she tentatively skitters down and across
    the wall, leaving no webs, no trace

father, I am too frightened to sleep

    will the spider crawl over my bed?
    will she wave her furry tentacles
    before my closed eyes, before inserting
    her jaws into pale skin and injecting her
    paler venom?

    will she leave a mark this night, a token
    of her gratitude for a dry
    safe place, hidden in the concrete eaves
    of my apartment?

    will she leave a bundle of her children behind
    when she goes —

father, there is a spider

what shall I do?

## The Lost Bunny Shrine of Annandale

It ended, as all good things end, in the toilet. Parts of it did, anyway. Parts of me, I mean. But I'm getting ahead of myself.

It was a hot August night. There were five of us. Initially. Mike (that's me), Matt, another guy named Matt,

Brian, and Dave. Yeah, two Matts. It got too confusing at times, so we just called the one Matt, the one from Ohio, by his nickname "Mischief." He was a troublemaker alright. Always carried a black and yellow backpack around for some reason.

As was typical, the five of us were sitting on the floor of the dorm commons room, surrounding two or three Talisman boards and extensions, with lots and lots of beer. Empty pizza boxes. Brian's stereo was blasting Metallica from our open dorm room. As I said, typical for us. Heavy metal, lots of beer, roleplaying and board games, wacky backy, a few acid trips here and there…and not a jock strap between us. We had a running joke, that you'd have to be crazy to go out with any of us. First question we ever asked any girl who dated a friend was, in fact, "Are you crazy?" Of course, I'd dated before. So had my roommate. In fact, the previous academic year we'd been dating twins who were probably just as crazy as us. I hadn't gotten anywhere with her, though. Just as well.

Now, on this particular evening, the end of a hot day at the end of August, there we were…the final night on a mostly empty campus with no upperclassmen but ourselves around (we thought), in the middle of Upstate with very, very little to do. The beer was mostly gone. Classes hadn't started. We were bored with the game, since we had played it basically every weekend the previous year.

"Hey, guys."

We looked up from the board game. Matt had just come back inside from a cig break out on the 3rd floor fire escape.

"Yeah, 'sup?"

"Let's go check out the new freshmen dorms."

Mischief snorted. "Now?"

"Yeah. Heard some of the international students were pretty hot."

"Oh?"

"Yeah, I met this cute guy from France…"

"Oh la la…"

"And some women, too…"

"Now you got my attention."

"Mischief, you gonna move?" Brian said. He was sitting on the floor, leaning back on one elbow and idly picking at discarded pizza slice crusts in a mostly empty pizza box.

"Dude, in a minute. Hey, anybody interested?"

There were a couple minutes of noncommittal shrugging and looking back and forth among the rest of us. It wasn't cool to be the first to admit we were bored and wanted to check out freshmen. But if girls were involved…

"Hey, anybody want a mudslide?" I blurted out.

"Uh…" was the general response.

"Dude," Brian said, propping himself up with both elbows now, "'sa fucksa mudslide?"

"Kahlua, Bailey's, and vodka," I said.

They all looked at me.

"That a girl's drink or something?" Brian smirked.

"Uh…"

Mischief shrugged. "If it's got vodka, sounds good to me."

"Bri?"

"Yeah, OK, me, too, I guess."

"Dave?"

Dave nodded. "I remember when I made mudslides a couple years ago. You know, the most important thing about mixing…"

"Matt?"

Matt shrugged and gave a thumb's up. He popped another cig out of a pack and went back out on the balcony.

The rest went back to the game, chatting about their supposed sexual conquests, while I got the drinks ready. Talk about sex always made me uncomfortable. Just about to be seniors, and I was still a virgin. Last thing I wanted them all to know then.

A short while later, after a couple of mudslides, everybody was feeling pretty toasted. I mean, toasted. The windows were open all the way, and guys were taking their shirts off. I had already changed into a tank top. No AC in the dorm. Brick building. Fourteen-foot-tall ceilings. No screens in the windows, either. Old school.

"Dude, pink?" Matt asked me.

I looked down at my shirt. "Yeah. It's the only clean one I got right now."

Matt raised an eyebrow and looked around the room. "Oh, come on, now. I don't know if I can control myself with so many half-naked men around..."

"Oh, yeah," Mischief lisped, running a hand down his side. "You know I turn you on."

"Oh, ew," Matt said, laughing.

"So..." Brian started.

"Yeah," Matt said. "You guys up for some freshmen?"

"Freshwomen?" Mischief corrected.

"Speak for yourself," Matt half-lisped.

Dave cut in, "Yeah, I remember the last time I was with a freshman. She was like, oh, wow, your..."

"We gonna go just like this?" I interrupted. "What time's...do we bring anything?"

"Wait a sec," Brian said. He ducked into our dorm room.

Mischief started putting his shirt back on, saying, "We can't go out like this, anyways."

Brian came back with a six-pack cardboard holder. "Not much, but I had a couple bottles of Zima and lemon-beer-something."

"Yech."

"What. Nothing wrong with Zima."

My head was already on the verge of swimming from the mudslides, but I said nothing. At least two of the other four were probably swimming, too, but nobody would ever admit that. Well, almost nobody.

"Dude, I am like soooo wasted..."

"Dave, you barely had half a glass."

"No, man, it was like...I had a lot, I can really hold my liquor. Like, this one time in Germany..."

At this point, another dorm mate, Bill came up the stairs into the room, followed by two of his friends. They'd just gotten back from their part-time jobs doing...ah, whatever. I never asked.

"Hey, what's going on?" Bill asked.

"We're heading out to..."

"Dave you're so full of..."

"Bill, dude, where'ya been..."

"Hey, I got a couple beers in the fridge, too, why don't I..."

"Freshmen? Hell, yeah..."

"Gotta change first..."

There were so many people now, I started losing track of the conversation. Conversations. At some point, we started heading down the stairs and out the building en masse. There were six or seven people now. Or was it eight? I was feeling pretty buzzed and wishing I had taken my contact lenses out.

"Alright, the motley crew is all here."

"Yeah, calling doctor love, baby..."

"Dave, that's KISS."

"Oh, yeah. I remember when I saw..."

We were a motley bunch, all right. The closest one of us to jock-dom, Mischief, in a Cleveland Indian T-shirt with a red bandana tied around his head, pirate-style. Dave, in a black trench coat, despite the heat, long hair and horn-rimmed glasses. Bill, in a high school band jacket with three letters sewn on the back surrounding a saxophone. Me, in a pink tank top and cut-off jeans. Matt, also in a tank top but with an open collar flared out, cuffs-rolled back, silk button-down shirt. Brian, looking like Alice Cooper if he wore a black fedora. Bill's roommate was also there, and one or two of their friends who had apparently tagged along. I never did figure out their names.

We left the old red and brown brick, ivy-covered dorm building of Stone Row and headed across campus, arguing Talisman strategy and debating music lyrics the whole way. First we walked along a paved walkway dimly-lit with overhead cheap fluorescent outdoor lamps. Then straggled down outside concrete staircases and onto a tiled outdoor patio, the only cafeteria on campus to the right. Facing the cafeteria was a long brick wall topped in concrete, beyond which lay the Lawn, where (we hoped) we would gather in a tent to graduate at the end of the year.

There, sitting on the wall under a flickering outdoor light made of black plastic and aluminum, was a group of female students.

"Dude, freshmen?" Mischief whispered to me.

I shrugged. No idea. I thought they looked older.

"No guys, Matt, sorry," Brian snickered.

Matt giggled. "I'll manage."

Mischief turned to us. "Leave this to me. Check it out."

We slowed our pace as a group as Mischief walked ahead, taking out a pack of cigarettes from a rolled up shirtsleeve.

"Hey, guys, what's up?" he asked with a slightly smarmy smile.

We let out a collective sigh. Great pickup line.

Cigarettes were shared. The beer came out. So did the Zima. It turned out they were international students, most from Russia or Serbia. Some had entered as freshman, some as sophomores. Most were 20 or 21 and had come for a half a year exchange program. When I was a freshman I had had a Serbian friend, who taught me a curse phrase in Serbian about mothers and goats before he had transferred to a school with a better tennis team. Probably not entirely useful a phrase in this situation, I reflected.

The conversation rambled on. I hung around the back of the group, nursing a Zima that Brian had thrust into my hands. Matt was standing even further back, chain-smoking Camel Lights. Mischief had zeroed in on one particular student, a tall blond who spoke the best English. I could tell that most of her group was uncomfortable; they had stood up, half-turned their backs to us, crossed their arms, not entirely willing to make eye contact. I couldn't blame them. I felt almost the same.

About ten minutes into the group "we don't really know you but are too reluctant and/or bored to leave" interaction, the topic of sports came up. One of the exchange students was thinking of joining the women's volleyball team for the fall term.

I had played volleyball in intramural sports each year. Sensing an opportunity, I plucked up my courage and gave it my best shot.

"So, you like volleyball?"

"Yes."

Well, that was less than ideal.

I thrust one hand in a ripped half-jeans pocket in what I hoped was a casual gesture. Taking a sip from my bottle, I tried again.

"So, uh, how long have you played?"

She paused. "In the high school, I played for some years. Three years."

Short brown hair. Same height as me, sharp cheekbones, straight jawline. God, she was gorgeous.

"Um, what posi...position did you play?"

She looked at me. "Position?"

"Yeah, uh, what's your specialty?"

She shrugged. "Nothing. I like to spike. And serve."

"Yeah, that's cool. I'm no good at blocking, but I like to serve."

"I see."

At that point, Mischief came over. Saved. Good thing; my head had started spinning again.

"Hey, we're all gonna head into the Enchanted Forest. Whaddya say?"

The Enchanted Forest. It was a strip of trees between the freshman dorms and the campus gymnasium, dotted with random abstract sculptures made by an artist who lived on campus. At least I think so. I wasn't an art major, but Brian swore up and down that it was a former part-time professor who had gone insane. That would figure.

"Matt, it's too dark…"

"No problem," he replied, yanking out a flashlight from a sidepocket of his backpack. "I always keep my maglight with me, remember?" He smacked it against one hand. "Good in a fight, too."

"What are you now, some kind of survivalist?" I laughed.

"Hey," someone spoke up, "how about the bunny shrine?"

The international students were now looking back and forth at each other, speaking rapidly.

The blond (whose name turned out to be Tiina) asked finally, "What is the bunny shrine?"

"It's a post. You know, a piece of wood, stuck in the ground. About yay high." Mischief gestured with his hand. "A couple of students had this pet rabbit, and they took pictures of him and buried him in the forest a while ago."

"Yeah," Bill added. "I ran into it by accident when we were freshmen."

"So…you want us to…go find this with you?"

"Sure. Why not?"

"Oh. Well, OK."

Now something like a dozen people, we started walking down the paved slope from the cafeteria's outside patio space to the road that separated the two halves of the campus. A small Episcopalian chapel stood across the road diagonally on the left. Directly in front, another newly paved road sloping downward, wide enough for just one car. This road had been unpaved, dirt and rock, when we were all freshmen. It ran down past the chapel and swept around to the left, past the original freshman dorms which hung on the edge of a ravine. The gym was up another slight slope to the right. In between the gym and the old freshman dorms...the Enchanted Forest, which took you straight into the ravine if you weren't careful.

"So," I said to the brunette, as we all continued to drink and smoke and scope each other out. "What's your favorite music?" Her name escaped me. Maybe I had forgotten to ask.

"Music?" she said absentmindedly, apparently trying to overhear a conversation between two of her friends in another language.

"Yeah, you know. Favorite band?"

"I like Beatles."

"Thass cool," Dave interrupted from behind us, appearing out of nowhere. "I remember this time when I met John Lennon."

Another voice behind us, Matt. "Lennon was shot in 1980. What were you, 8?" he scoffed, flicking ash from a cig onto the ground.

"Yeah, I was 8. My dad," Dave said happily, drunkenly, to the brunette and her two friends, none of whom seemed remotely interested, "my father, he's like this big name..."

"Shut up and drink."

We gathered on the edge of the Forest, where a footpath ran through it, connecting the road to the freshman dorms and the gymnasium. As the confused and mixed language conversations continued, Mischief turned off the footpath and crashed into the trees, calling out for us to follow him. After two or three minutes the lights from the road and the gym on either side of us had dimmed. We were only aware that the land was slowly sliding downward again and that there was a small stream ahead of us.

"It's too dark. Let's go back," somebody shouted.

"Taken care of!" Mischief's voice came back to us. We saw a light bobbing up and down ahead of the group, which was now stumbling ahead. Some of our new companions began to hold hands so they wouldn't get lost. I was tempted. The sudden exertion of hiking in the woods had made my head swim, and I started sweating.

"Turn at the stream!" somebody hollered. Bill?

The light bobbed again, then jerked to the left. The group followed, now in twos and sometimes single-file, as the darkness and pine needles surrounded us. There was no path. I felt branches slap against my cheeks, swatted them away and got sap on my fingers. We seemed to be going in circles. At least twice we walked past the same strange metal sculpture, some sort of scorpion with a rusted round saw blade for a body...another that looked like a flute player made out of old Coke cans...For a moment I lost sight of whoever had been in front of me, then I caught sight again...A pressure around my neck...Matt, holding my tank top from behind as we all continued our search for a piece of wood commemorating a student's dead pet rabbit.

"Dude, let up. I can't breathe..."

"Mike, all's I can see is your pink shirt..."

I turned around. He had given up trying to smoke and was holding my shirt with one hand and a zippo with the other. I turned back. Where was everybody? There, ahead, a few people.

More crashing through low branches, random shouting. The air felt dense. Sweat crept down into my eyes. Had I dropped the bottle? Where the light? I stumbled forward, occasionally yanked backward by Matt. Where did everybody go? My head was swimming again, my body growing heavy, like being underwater...it got darker...

"Here!"
Finally.
"Over here! I found it!"
I pushed through yet more pine branches and stepped into a clearing of sorts. There, surrounded by seven or eight people who had made it that far, was the Lost Bunny Shrine. I heard the crashing through trees of more people behind me as I approached. Matt still had his hand on my shirt. He was breathing hard. Stopping, he shoved a hand in his front pants pocket and retrieved an inhaler.

"Dude, you okay?" I asked.

He nodded, then shook his head. "Don't matter." And took a puff.

I turned back to the Shrine. Mischief had handed his maglight to Brian and was retrieving something from his black and yellow backpack. A flash of light, another. A camera?

"It's...it's real," one of the international students murmured.

"Yeah, see!" Mischief crowed. He stood up from his camera-man crouch. "Come on and take a look!"

The post was, as Mischief had said, somewhere between waist- and chest-high. A 4x4 with some sort of metal fence on top. On each of the four sides, there were flaps, cut-outs with tiny handles that you could pull up to see faded photographs. One side read "Mr. Bunny: We loved him" and gave dates, some time in October 1983.

I looked up and realized I had been squatting. Then I fell over.

When I woke up, I was on the floor of my dorm room, sweating in the sunlight, dressed only in underwear. Between my roommate Brian's bed and mine. IBM PS/2 and stereo set on my desk in front of me. The box fan in the wooden window frame was turned on low. A gentle breeze washed over me as I looked around without getting up. What...

An arm flopped down from my roommate's bed. It wasn't Brian's. What...

I heard a light footfall from behind me. Rolling slightly to one side, I tried to look back to see who it was, and couldn't quite do it.

"Easy, now, easy," a voice whispered. It was Dave. He had a plastic gallon jug filled with water, which he set down on a desk behind my roommate's bed.

"What...what happened?" I managed.

Dave shook his head. "Man, I haven't seen this much..."

"Dave, what happened?"

"We had to help you back to the dorm, dude. You kind of made a mess in the bathroom sink. But it's okay, it got cleaned up already."

I groaned. My head had started pounding.

"Is..."

"Hey, take it easy," Dave said again, pouring water into a somewhat clean red plastic party cup as I sat up, slowly, propping my back against my bed. I accepted the cup, gratefully, and drained it in one gulp.

"What time is it?" I asked.

Dave glanced at his watch. "Quarter past 11. I stayed on the couch in the common room, you know. I've never felt so bad for..."

Somebody was behind me on my bed. I turned, and there was Matt, still sleeping, but fully dressed, his silk shirt crumpled and reeking of Camel Light.

"Dave, why..."

"Yeah, man, I totally saw it," Brian's voice came from the other bed. I looked over and saw the owner of the arm. The brunette from last night, lying on her stomach next to Brian, who was stretching his arms and yawning. He banged his right arm against the wall and cursed. Neither had shirts on.

"You what?" I said.

Dave refilled my cup and giggled. "Nothing, man, nothing."

"No, 'strue, dude. Matt totally stuck his dick into your..."

"Say what!" I nearly shouted.

Both Dave and Brian laughed. Behind me, Matt began to stir, coughing and turning over.

"Nah, just winding you up, dude," Brian confessed, massaging his companion's back. She hummed and reached up to hold his hand.

"I told you, dude," Dave said, shaking his head. "You were totally out of it. Even Katya had to help drag you up here."

"Kat...?"

She opened one eye and looked at me.

I stared, and then shook my head.

"You guys, you all crazy," she said, smiled, and went back to sleep.

## My Bloody

You once told me — I loved the idea of being in love

       I loved the idea of loving
      and there was a difference
      but I was too selfish and
         thought too much of you to care

Don't ever say I never loved you — you did

        you loved the feeling of love
      the way it made you feel
      special content wanted loved
         but not needed you were too special

I changed my mind — no, it changed for me

        you didn't want to change you
      it just happened and you went
      along, long line of names and faces
         but I wanted to be more than another efface

And you weren't good enough for me — you were right

        I deserved more, more than a lie
      a series of lies, not lies mistruths
      deceits our bodies played on us in front of our
         backs like shadows on your bedroom wall

  flickering,

## Notes From the Nineties

intransient,

melting,

— gone —

## Pockets

Peter was immediately attracted to her. She wasn't particularly physically attractive: tall and slender, pale and wispy, almost a wraith. She liked to wear leather and black. She dyed her hair black as well, but if you looked close enough, you could see the reddish roots struggling to push their tips above ground just long enough to let the world know that something was being covered up. She always smiled, a pleasant smile, though sometimes she could add facial expressions to change its connotation, when it suited her, and it suited her well.

He occasionally passed her on his way to the Eastern Quads, always when it was windy and cool and clear. They approached from opposite directions in the fields, bypassing the blacktop pathways in favor of treading upon the stilted greenery with patches brown and worn-down, slightly rolling hilltops. She would spread her arms out as she drifted through the grass, spreading wide to the breeze her dark cloak into which her body seemed to melt. Her hair flew back, at once revealing her pale face and yet concealing it. She had to fling back the blackness from her eyes, and, spreading her wings once more, she would smile as she floated past. Peter would slow his amble, hands thrust deeply into his pockets, as if he were hiding in the button-up red wool jacket, and gaze after her, at the phantom in space, oblivious and completely aware of her surroundings. Then he would turn and wander in the direction he was originally heading, his attention lingering upon the image in the fields.

The same the rest of the semester, almost on a weekly basis: she with billowing cloak and pale skin and he with his hands in his pockets, fumbling with pieces of paper or keys or little pebbles, whatever was in his pockets at the time. The pockets reassured him; his arms, drawn in close to his sides, folded his body in upon itself, protecting him from the probing of passersby. His hands couldn't stop fidgeting. He sometimes took them out, pretending to blow upon them for warmth, rubbing them against each other, feeling the knuckles on his left hand, massaging the fleshy part of the upper palm with his right thumb. Then he would thrust the hands back into the pockets, taking refuge in the warm darkness of the wool.

81

After a time Peter took to smoking, casually at first. He didn't really know what made him decide to buy a pack of cigarettes, but he had a good excuse. Smoking gave his hands something to do, holding a Marlboro between his first two fingers as his other hand gripped a bottle of indeterminate beer, walking about with his jacket brazenly unbuttoned. He saw her at the parties he went to every weekend. She always wore a black knee-length skirt and black stockings, which only further highlighted her smiling white visage. She wasn't alone in wearing black, but she was one of the few who stood out. Her height, for one thing; at the same time her litheness enabled her to slip in and out of crowds like a shadow. She alone among the party-goers did not smoke or drink, as if she, out of all those who sought release in the embrace of intoxication, found solace in sobriety.

He usually clung to the back walls, numbly quivering a leg to the pulsating beat of the dance music, watching the mostly drunken dancers whirling about, jumping up and down or merely swaying in place with solemn expressions. Peter imagined that all eyes were upon him, he felt trapped, hopelessly pinned against the wall, yet he didn't want to leave. The unwillingness to leave became an inability to leave — he could have always gone back to his tiny room and worked on papers or read or listened to music, but while he listened again to the music he had heard a thousand times and could quote by heart, he would picture the party, he could see those in his classes enjoying themselves, and he would berate himself for not being there.

And so there he was, constantly nursing cold, foul-tasting cheap beer and pretending to absentmindedly take drags on cigarette after cigarette, making believe that he enjoyed the company of people who were not his friends and who never would be his friends. And he looked for her.

Whenever she was there, Peter could scarcely take his gaze from her. He followed her every movement, never bothering to conceal his interest. Sometimes she would glance around the room, and, noticing his stare, flash a smile that reached her mischievous eyes, and just as quickly look away. He was enthralled; he wanted to talk to her, to find out who she was and what she believed, why she dressed like a dark angel — but he couldn't bring himself to eliminate this image. He was desperate to reach for her, but he dared not.

Peter would always lean back against the brown stained wall, elbow to elbow with similarly-clad students with cigarettes and drinks, bottling his thoughts as he chugged beer after beer. After each night of indecision and self-isolation, he would shove his hands back into his pockets, once more playing with a lighter or cigarettes broken in half or folded bits of paper, and plod off alone to his cave.

His room was, by itself, unremarkable. Two walls were brick, part of the original hundred-year-old building. Of the other two, one faced the main square of campus and provided a lovely view of a smokestack forever belching voluminous grey clouds high above the courtyard. There was one small rectangular window in this wall which rattled with the wind and let in cold drafts. The remaining wall adjoined the bathroom, allowing the various gurgles and drips to inform him whether or not the shower and toilet were in use. The ceiling was about fourteen feet high, permitting any heat in the room to escape above comfortable living space. To offset this, he had constructed a loft, which stood eight feet above the floor and the cold work space surrounding his desk and was built solidly enough to withstand an earthquake — or at least the vibrations caused by one neighbor's fondness for moving furniture late at night and another's jackhammer of an electric bass.

The loft was actually simple to build: four two-by-fours, two to the left and two to the right, comprised the legs, with the corner closet as the middle support of the giant L. Ascending four-foot lengths straddled one pair of legs for a ladder leading up to the platform that awkwardly extended a few inches too far over the ladder, making it difficult though not impossible to get into bed. Peter had nailed two leftover pieces at the top for hand-holds, drilled a hole in the other side of the loft for his stereo plug. He had even strung a cotton rope from the loft to the outside and back again for an indoor clothesline. Books adorned the otherwise staid walls of the room, most of them either read so often that he knew them by heart or not read at all and merely there for show.

Next to the door he hung a charcoal drawing from an aborted art class. Copied from a Rembrandt, it depicted an angel preventing Abraham from sacrificing Isaac, instead offering a lamb caught in a rose bush. It was one of the few art ventures with whose results it could be said he was pleased, though it was but a copy.

He spent his days with books and money in a store three floors directly beneath his room. The job paid him little, offered scant hours and often drew thinly-veiled bitterness from classmates, but it was better than not working at all, and, frankly, he needed the pittance. How could he complain, spending all morning and nighttime hours in the same building, with only a change in altitude the difference? It was like home at work, and he never complained about the store or his role. It did, after all, enable him to buy the necessities for the parties of Friday and Saturday.

She would come into the store almost every day — at least, every day that Peter worked there, it seemed. She appeared more human inside the store, flitting from bookshelf to bookshelf, leafing through tomes of "magic" and the occult, never buying any of them. One afternoon she bought a few art supplies, acrylic paints and brushes, some charcoal and a drawing pad, and he found himself talking to her at the register. They talked briefly, an inane conversation about art in general and the cost of it. She said her name was Rosemary — "But most of my friends call me Rose," she said smiling.

"Peter," he said, managing a small smile. She smiled again, and it became easier for him to return it. He watched her leave the store and return to phantasmal form, gliding into the square between dorms as the wooden door slowly closed upon her image. He kept his eyes on the closed door for a moment, guarding the image in his mind, knowing there was no way he could forget.

During the following week Peter performed his duties faithfully and checked his impatience as the days passed. Friday never came quickly enough, nor did it last long enough. A fleeting moment of indecision each week, maybe two: he anxiously waited through the hours for apprehension to peak, then inevitably slumped as anxieties were spent and slipped away to his retreat to recuperate. He had convinced himself that this was an unchangeable ritual, Sisyphus constantly rolling a keg up a mountain only to have it tumble backwards again into the brine. Not only was it unchangeable, he thought that somehow subconsciously he did not wish to change it. It had become easy to accomplish the same moment every Friday, encouraged by the clockwork occurrence of a party in the same crowded, smoke-filled dark chamber. His right hand now seemed to instinctively form the shape of a brown bottle, his left ready to poise a cancer stick in front of his lips. Recently, he had begun to keep his hands out his pockets as long as possible before the jacket began to feel light and he was compelled to weigh down the emptiness to prevent himself from drifting forward into the throng. He could view the scene with an increasing sense of detachment, at the same time feeling closer to it. But not this Friday.

Friday did come. The crowd was there, and so was Peter, in the back. Against the wall, beer in right hand, cigarette smoke encircling his head. Peter was feeling closer yet distanced from the swelling, swaying numbers around him. The swaying dancers filled his vision. He finished another bottle. And she seemed to approach him in a haze of second-hand smoke. Rosemary's face highlighted in the cloudy darkness, she smiled and relaxed her shoulders as he said hello.

"Hey, are you...?" she started.

"Yes," Peter heard himself interrupt. "Would you like to go someplace else?"

She tilted her head to examine him. "Sure," she said easily, smiling again. The smile reached her eyes, which, so close, he could see were blue.

He extended an arm behind her as if to usher her out the side door; she hooked her left arm around his, escorting him into the square outside. Peter began to speak, but her pose told him that she did not desire conversation, as she directed him towards the East Quads.

Instead, his face feeling warm, he turned towards the store. She followed, matching his uneven pace with her long stride. Walking around the end of the building, they ascended the three flights of stairs to his door, which he opened unsteadily. Letting go of his arm, she caught sight of the loft as he fairly staggered into the room. He slowly turned the dimmer switch on a small desk lamp underneath the loft. She silently twirled in the middle of the room in the increasing intensity, her arms above her head like a priest at Eucharist, blessing the consecrated dwelling.

She stopped at looked at him; Peter blinked, and she whispered, "It's beautiful." Letting her black cloak slide down her white arms onto the floor, she backed away, tantalizing. Peter stood still, an image of flowing grass fluttering through his hazy thoughts. He felt his hands slip into his jacket pockets. He felt foolish.

"So, uh, so, you...like it?" he tried. Dumb. He felt a pounding in his throat. His tongue felt swollen and thick. She smiled and tilted her head as she ran her left hand up the ladder. She looked up at the plywood platform. "How do you get up there?" she asked.

"Uh, hold on," he stuttered, clumsily taking the jacket off, holding onto the sleeve as long as he could before dropping it onto the chair in front of the desk. With his right hand gripping one post, he swung himself around the corner and onto the makeshift ladder. Scampering up the two-by-fours, his head lunged down toward the platform, stopping short of hitting the wood. Quickly jerking his head upright, temples throbbing, he turned around atop the mattress. Looking down at her, Peter could see the swell of pale breasts peeking above her black leather bodice. He smiled, she smiled back. "See?" he said. "It's not too tough."

"Okay," she replied. Finding a foothold on the bottom rung, she reached up with slender arms, black-nailed hands, and began to climb. He backed up, dragging the sheets with him, a thin rip slitting the fitted cover, as her breasts appeared over the edge and landed on the pillow. Black hair parting, her eyes smiling, He paused. She stifled a giggle as he leaned to offer a hand. With a final push, she lurched forward, knocking him backward, falling on top of his outstretched torso. He tasted perfume and hair spray. She raised her head with parted lips, drawing the hair away from his face as he propped himself with an elbow. Eyes focusing on the white face before his, he felt a silly grin spreading. He sat upright, too quickly, his head spinning, and she grabbed his shoulders.

"Are you all right?" she asked, sounding concerned. Cleared his throat and nodded. "Yeah, I'm...fine," he said, looking up right into blue-sky eyes. Her gaze shifted down, just a bit, and her lips seemed to move almost imperceptibly up and down. He felt a sudden pressure below the waist. Small beads of perspiration dotted his hairline. "I..." She said nothing but continued gazing intently. He felt himself slipping forward, felt the impression of wet, saline fingertips of flesh, warm stale breath closing around him. His hands extended outward, reaching, as he listed to the left, mouthing hunger.

*His left hands meets nothingness, his feet sliding back, down, wrenching his knees as the warmth is pulled away. His right hand flails, catching threads, his knees unfolding and projecting him down, down, as his left hand waves. A cry from above, from pain or shock, and a hand grips his wrist. His neck connects with clothesline, one foot shooting up and landing on the plywood. His right hand pulls toward him, and he hears another cry from above in anger. He tries to open his eyes: a white image or is it black appears over him, and he longs for his pockets. The image speaks, the pain in his neck explodes as the line snaps, and he pitches. He hears one crash, two, things falling on top of each other, glass shattering in a corner, then a distant thud, sound of a body touching down. White and black shadows descend upon him. His hand hurts, he tastes salt. Silky cloth flutters over his eyes, and he closes them.*

Peter awoke upon the loft to the sound of an electric fan near the window and construction men outside. Lifting a hand to his eyebrows, blocking out the white ceiling, he massaged his sinuses and rolled on his right side. The clock read twelve noon. He rolled back onto his stomach and buried his forehead in the cool pillow, fetally curling his nakedness. A dream? He had no recollection of returning after the party. His alarm went off—was it Monday already? He felt the downstairs call him, and he knew he must respond.

His body groaned as he got to his knees and prepared for the climb down. Pulling the twisted yellow sheets with him, he swung his ankles over the end of the loft, touching his toes to rough wood. His wrists felt enflamed, his toenails nicked the edges of the two-by-fours, but he made it safely to the floor. Looking only at his feet, holding a palm to his burning forehead, Peter stumbled to the dresser and tried to peer into a small mirror. He felt a rush of hot fluid from below, thorax convulsing, and flung open the door. Not yet, please, not yet, the bathroom's right...

Only a few drops spattered around the bowl, the rest projecting into the calm, blue water. A light cool breeze wafted from the porcelain, his hands and elbows on the bowl's lip, his face flushed. Eyes firmly shut, he reached toward the lever to siphon the bile away. His stomach quietly gurgled, his abdomen relaxed as his body slowly straightened. A few sheets from the toilet paper roll cleared the area of trace elements.

Holding on to the stall door, he shuffled to the sink and turned the faucets on. Bending over to splash water on his face, he pressed his fingers against his bony cheeks and hollow eye sockets. He carefully raised his head, huge hands covering his face in front of the wall mirror above the sink. Dragging his fingers through his hair, Peter opened his eyes and saw himself. Then he remembered. Something from the previous night — or was it two? what was it? — a number. A piece of paper with a phone number. He had folded it, put it in his jacket for safe-keeping. His jacket never lost anything.

He returned to the room in search of the jacket. There it was, draped over the brown chair like a deflated sigh. He found his slacks from the day before, hanging from the clothesline where it always had been. Took out a crumpled pack of Marlboro, lit a broken cigarette and coughed noisily. Slouched in the chair, reaching into one of the pockets with his free hand, Peter mentally drew her face in the air. The image wavered, his hand touched nothing. His hand jumped nervously into the other pocket, he turned the pockets inside out, flipped the jacket upside down and shook it. The image disappeared, the cigarette burned out.

The pockets were empty.

## Enamour Fati

Why
does it take so long for you
to know what is important to you;
why do we have to learn from our mistakes

    (Hoping it hadn't been a mistake I
    give myself over to a long embrace
    on a cold night of candles
    and lukewarm conversational asides)

Everything
reminds me of something else
everyone resembles someone I have known
or wanted to know or didn't or never will

    (giving someone a hug is more tiresome
    than receiving, especially if beforehand
    the realization it will not be reciprocated
    caffeinates senses to higher detachment)

Is
it Prescience that only works in gloomy
retrospect, remarkably accurate for a memory;
but only if you can see it coming

    (wishing holding you for ever never works
    only threading time through brittle fingers
    and when it unravels the sensation of
    us slipping away does not upset as much)

Fate
and love are said to intertwine,
as if each owes the other a debt of conscience;
but I owe neither more than cursory shrugs

      (Forever this, relative to those before,
      may seem a long time           to you
      I once loved your ways, your destiny)

      No fond farewells, love, just our final
           hello.

Frank

The difference is, I lie for a reason. I mean, compared to Frank. He's just a damn liar. I'm a damn good liar. No. That's not true. I did lie, of course. But it was the truth.

See, no matter what I tell you, you'll never believe me. No matter how I explain it, no matter what I say or do, I *know* you won't be satisfied. You want logical explanations for every action, every word, every thought...everything. You look for conspiracies, subversions, subterfuge—and then you get...me. You're angry, frustrated that it's so simple. I make your job easy. I tell you what happened, who did it and why, and yet you say I lied. So why not lie? I mean, you don't really want the truth, in the end.

So, the truth? I had to do it. You'll never believe me...maybe even call me crazy but...Nobody helped me, no one convinced me, coaxed me, coerced me. That's not a lie. I just thought about it for a long time—not really that long, actually, but a decent while—and then I knew what I had to do. No. I lied. But there's a reason, of course.

It was easy, really. Everything was easy. He was always open, trusting, so trusting, liked to walk out in the open among the crowds, even refused bodyguards. I'm a pretty good shot with a...of course, you don't need to be a good shot that close. I just pushed through the crowds, all calm, very calm. Slid it from my pocket, pulled the trigger, and a nice red stain appeared on his left jacket pocket. I didn't hear anything, just squeezed again and again. Something came out of his mouth as he fell back and...yeah, I guess I sorta got carried away. Didn't mean to get anybody else. They just happened to get in the way.

Well, I'm not saying I wanted to do it. No, it's true. He was a good man, decent, honest, smart. He knew what had to be done, no doubt about it. But he couldn't. Not his fault, not entirely...they wouldn't let him, they never would...have. Just like before, just like when Jack was alone at the top. Finally get someone young, energetic, willing to work for us, and then they get in the way. It wasn't his fault, wasn't in the wrong, but...they wouldn't help. Tried to gut his programs, tried to...something had to be done. But you all were paralyzed. Scared. Cowards.

Nobody wanted, no one had the guts to do what had to be done. No one, but me.

I knew that it was quote-unquote wrong. I knew I would be punished, maybe killed, executed, for sure. But that didn't stop me. Nothing mattered, but that. Didn't matter what was wrong or right...no, it's true. How can you justify murder? Because I can't. Not trying to. Murder, killing someone, anyone, even for a good cause...well, it just shouldn't be done. Even I know that, even after all I went through over there, all the sacrifices I made for us all. Sometimes you just have to forget wrong and right, ignore what they say, everybody else. Sometimes you just have to. Do it. Not because it's right, not because you want a place in history. Just. *Because.*

You call me crazy. My lawyer says I'm crazy. Pleads insanity. But he lies. He says I don't know the difference between wrong and right...but he lies. I'm guilty. That's the reason. No question about it. I deserve punishment. Not for doing something wrong, no. But that's all right. I'll be the first guilty man accused for the wrong reason of doing something wrong. It doesn't matter. I'll deal. You'll be satisfied. The state will be satisfied, the people will think...

Well, whatever they think is fine. You'll see. It'll work out all right. I *know* it'll work out all right. It worked out just fine before, with Jack and Lyndon. They knew what had to be done. So did I. I have no excuses for what I did...just a reason.

No. That's not true. I'm a liar.

## Asleep Came the Vision of I

I dreamt the Sistine Chapel, I
shut tight my eyes: swirl first and
first-born in a round. Arms clasp in
firm grasp, forearm to fore
arm, blues' and whites' whorl, a
rapid dilation from dome into
sphere. The Spirits-thrice keen.

The life tree appears, to center
the storm, stands rooted from
top to top. Ring around the rosy,
maids around the pole see
the ash's fall down, down,
but no ground.
                        Collide the worlds
and cracks that curl from finger
to wrist and flake in pearls of
blackest black, brightness most bright,
condemn the circular sky.

Rise above all, I swing here legs
crossed, these arms spread wide
upside down. Nine days nine nights;
Grim's eye bares wide, the design
to reveal its designer.
                        Two
Birds alight, I remember myself:
the blue in the blue, a whiteness of white,
the hands do not touch, the lone
center of I spreads barren.

# The Four Teeth of the Apocrypha

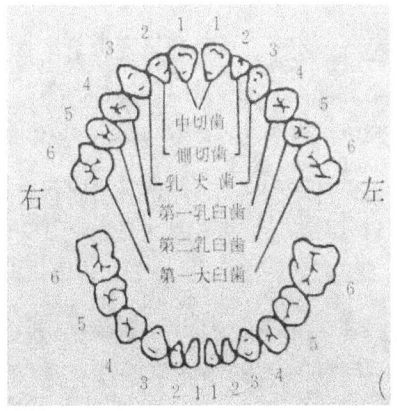

>                        *'Why, Cadmus, why*
> *Stare at the snake you've slain? You too shall be*
> *A snake and stared at.'*
>                             *...Gliding down*
> *Out of the sky Pallas appears and bids*
> *Him plough the soil and plant the serpent's teeth,*
> *From which a future people should arise.*

Brian Lewis, of 1202 South Ave, Ann Arbor, Michigan, aged 31, lay back uncomfortably in the dentist's chair while Dr. Paul Michaels, a greying man with small narrow glasses, breathed into Brian's closed eyelids and benumbed facial tissue, and this is what Brian envisioned:

He wakes up this morning with one arm dead asleep underneath his stomach, the other with a prickly sensation draped off the side of the bed and almost curled underneath the box frame. Slowly dragging the semi-functional arm over his head to the cubby-hole head rest, a still sleepy Brian tenderly touches the snooze button and pulls the entire black plastic alarm with bright orange LCD on top of his hair-entangled cranium.

Knocking the clock behind him onto the bed, Brian winces and then sighs. He rolls onto his back first, then lurches his feet onto the cold wood floor with his still-not-quite overweight a tad corpus in tow. Brian carefully pulls his long dark-brown hair back into a ponytail and wraps a red and yellow elastic band around three times. No time for a shower. The appointment is in fifteen minutes.

Brian quickly washes his face and his shoulders and underarms with a soapy hand cloth. Not that he needs to go the store today—in fact, he'd rather not spend any part of his day off in the comic book/miniatures store he must manage roughly 16 hours a day, 13 days on, one off. But appearances are unfortunately important for a noticeable, amiable six foot five bearded manager of a popular student hangout.

The shoulders were not necessary to clean, he reflects upon replacing the hand cloth on the rack, but, since he missed his morning yoga, maybe the warmth will loosen up his ever-tense neck muscles just a bit. Smoothing out his short beard, Brian reaches for his wireless wire-frame, lineless bifocals resting behind the sink faucets, which then allows him to discover where he last left his dresser. Wrinkled pants, hurriedly-smoothed out button-down shirt, and black work boots with steel tips all thrown on, Brian grabs his muddied black trench coat, deposits a large floppy hat upon his pulled back hair, and all but flies down Seventh Street on his mountain bike to the dentist's office.

Even though his eyes remained closed, Brian felt as if the dull white light emanating from above penetrated his eye sockets clear through to the back of his head. The dentist instructed Brian to clasp his hands beneath the gigantic blue tissue paper tablecloth spread across Brian's midsection from underneath the chin to his waist. Brian complied. He felt his fingers nervously slide his signet ring into a palm and begin to pass it back and forth as if juggling underwater. Briefly Brian wondered if this was noticeable to the dentist or his female assistant, but the two were intent upon discussing the local elementary school's soccer league tournament.

"That was a fine, fine game last weekend, I have to tell you," Dr. Michaels said conversationally to his nurse attendant. Brian still had his eyes firmly closed, but it seemed to him as if the dentist were carefully picking up the metal tools which lay in a small tray and examining them one at a time. Sounds from the ceiling satellite radio station seemed to diffuse through all parts of the room, randomly chosen songs from yesterday and today attempting to filter into his weakened mental resistance. Brian automatically rolled two ten-sided dice in his head and came up oh-six. Good, he thought, he would resist easily.

"How long did it go? Two overtimes?" the nurse asked. Brian pictured her for a second, the red-haired image of her picking up the drill and passing it to the dentist, then rearranging the remaining clinking silverware. One of her thighs pressed momentarily into Brian's left arm as he lay there waiting, and he felt a brief thrill; though he knew it was silly, he felt it nonetheless.

The hand of Dr. Michaels descended upon Brian. "Open up wide now, Brian," the rubber-gloved hand said into Brian's upper jaw. Brian complied again, and instantly felt three sharp pinpricks pinch his upper palate, the needles stabbing straight upwards into the inside of his nose. "Now, it doesn't get any more painful than this," Brian heard through the milky haze swimming inside his eyelids. "These will keep the swelling down."

Brian felt himself fidgeting and willed his body to calm down. His heart had started racing some time ago, despite his attempts at meditation. Without the proper music, and in a completely sanitized, wholly alien environment, he hadn't thought it would work anyway. Pain flared occasionally in his right bicep, crawling across his chest and into the other arm, from the shot half an hour previous...what he thought was half an hour...maybe it was a whole hour...or maybe ten minutes...

"How did Steven do?" the nurse asked, raising her voice a little too querulously, Brian thought. She leaned further into his arm.

"Not too bad, not too bad," the dentist replied. "He got one assist in the second period, I think. He didn't start last year, but he's playing with the eleven-year-olds now."

"Well," the nurse said, "they sure had nice weather for it."

"Yes, they did. Hear it's going to snow this weekend, so I guess we'd better appreciate the good weather while we have it."

The conversation stopped, and Brian took his ring off again underneath the big blue bib. Unsuccessfully he tried to ignore the quiet buzzle of ceiling radio sounds breaking through his stern facade.

"Okay, Brian," said Dr. Michaels, "We're going to start now. Elaine, could you rinse and suction the area, please."

The warmth at Brian's left receded, and a tube inserted itself between his incredibly fat bottom lip and his teeth. Water streamed forth into his mouth and was just as quickly suctioned back up again, he thought. A mild whirring noise began to his right as the dentist bent Brian's head backward and pried the jaws apart.

"All I want to do is be with you..." the dentist mumbled in a completely tone-deaf voice.

Brian sets foot in the squat red brick building with no windows, and begins to try to keep a steady heart rate. He decides at the last moment to go for local anesthesia for his wisdom teeth extraction. General will simply cost too much, and, he realizes, he's too scared to go under.

Brian manages to stay calm during the forty-minute wait in the outside office, nonchalantly thumbing month-old issues of *Time* and *Newsweek* and pointedly not looking at the television which looks down from a high corner perch. Once in a while, Brian looks at his wristwatch, but he has time. What is time, he ruminates while reading an article of the planned unmanned Mars probe, trying to devise a witty quip on the subject for his good-naturedly complaining workers at the store.

A voice from around a corner calls his name, and Brian sets down the magazine to follow. An off-white corridor, the third or fourth faux-wooden door to the left, he sees the green-blue plastic-looking chair and sits. The nurse has long, wavy red hair, and she talks about something as Brian sheds his coat and hat. He then realizes that laying back in the chair while still sporting a ponytail might turn out uncomfortable, so he reaches up and lets his hair down, pockets the elastic band. If the nurse notices his long hair, she says nothing about it.

"Okay, Brian," she says. Brian reads her name tag: Elaine.

"Okay, Brian," Elaine says, handing him a clear plastic clipboard with paper attached. "We just need you to read this and sign your initials in the blanks with exes next to them, okay?"

"Okay," he says, glancing down the list. The waiver form is fairly standard, he thinks, up to and including the sentence which reads:

"_____ 9. I understand that Dr. Michaels cannot be held responsible if I encounter a sudden coronary attack requiring immediate medical attention, either from reaction to anesthesia or from natural causes."

Brian looks up and asks pleasantly, "What does this part mean, 'coronary attack'?"

Elaine laughs and gives a short wave of the hand as she pulls out a cylindrical machine from in back of the chair. "Oh, that rarely happens, but, you know, if you were to have a heart attack during surgery, there's nothing we can do about it. It's happened once or twice elsewhere, but not here, but, you know, you don't have to worry about that."

"Uh, well, okay." He signs a short sharp BL down every badly xeroxed blank and hands the clipboard back.

She rolls up his right sleeve, leaving the machine on his left, takes his blood pressure, twice, three times, just to make sure. 137 over 90, she says, a bit high, but acceptable, probably just a little nervous tension. He agrees, nervously, with tension, and proceeds to pretend he has done this sort of thing half a dozen times already.

Just don't say to yourself, Brian says to himself, that you're presently paying a University of Michigan dentist four hundred some-odd dollars to turn your face into a scaled replica of the moon.

"Since your sleeve is already rolled up," Elaine says brightly, sneakily, "I might as well give you this now." She rubs a moistened cotton swab over a fleshy part of Brian's exposed arm, as he immediately says, "I hate shots."

"I know," Elaine says. "So do I." She then stabs him with a needle the size of the Sears Tower. It burns.

"Ahhh!" Brian exclaims. He clamps his mouth shut and closes his eyes as the burning sensation travels up his arm and across his chest. "That felt like a tetanus shot!"

"It's a shot of something called Decadron. It's a hormone produced by the brain, an antihistamine, to keep the swelling down."

Brian nods. Makes sense, he reasons, and says so. Elaine agrees, throwing away the needle tip, pushing back the machine, tidying up the counter top, doing something with some papers and manila envelopes. She starts telling him about what will happen after the surgery, when he has to deal with sutures and salt water rinses and check-ups, soft food for a couple of days and painkillers, maybe using a syringe to keep everything infection-free for a fast recovery.

"Dr. Michaels will be in soon to get you all numbed up," she says, opening the door and slipping out. "Okay?" She closes the door and he nods, closing his eyes, beginning to drift to strange elevator music in his head.

Brian felt a distinct pop in his lower right jawbone, and instinctively his tongue flapped over the wound. The tooth's crown had come clean off, he knew, thinking, *Now it's slice and dice time.* Any second now, he knew, the dentist's metal fingers would tear into his unprotected pink gums and gouge a deep gash into the tissue at the corner of his jaws. Rubber-gloved squeaks against the left side of his jaws informed Brian that Dr. Michaels was inserting something into his mouth; Brian's tongue tentatively explored, touched a cold hard square block, plastic, he surmised, wedged firmly between his molars.

"Bite down, please," Dr. Michaels said. Brian did.

"Okay, Brian," Dr. Michaels continued, reaching into Brian's mouth with another instrument, "now, you're probably going to hear some sounds. Don't worry, this is completely normal. It's just some sounds and some noise, nothing to worry about at all."

Brian felt Elaine shift at his left. He clasped his hands a bit tighter and tried to relax them, fiddling with his ring again. A pressure on his right side lower gum building, liquid began to fill the tiny pocket cavity between the right cheek and jaw.

"Suction there," the dentist mumbled. The tube drew the liquid away. A rough hand pulled back the flesh a bit, but Brian felt only the pressure and no pain. Another slight pressure at the gumline, and more liquid.

"Ease up a bit, Brian, so I can have more slack."

Brian understood, and attempted to force his mouth to close some, jutting forward the lower jaw in the process.

"That's better," Dr. Michaels said. Brian felt the hand again, this time grabbing hold of the corner of his mouth and yanking back the cheek from the jaws. A muscled line along Brian's upper lip stood out from the cheek, pulling the cartilage of his nose in that direction. Brian tried to grimace, then realized he couldn't because he had no control over his facial expressions. The tip of his nose seemed to extend outwards and upwards, turning back in upon itself. His heels alternately banged against the chair as Dr. Michaels' hand continued to further separate the flesh and cartilage from Brian's skull. The left side of Brian's nose now spread approximately above his right eyeteeth.

"Aahhh," he said in a muffled voice.

"Sorry about that, Brian," Dr. Michael said. "More noise, that's all it is." He pulled on the skin harder.

Beyond the cold slab of his office chair, Brian hears dim voices up and down the hallway, like bees droning, or library florescent lights. His eyed closed, waiting for the doctor to arrive, he stretches his calf muscles, tries to drift down into himself, to lower his pulse.

*Hello, hello...*
   *hello, is there anybody...*

"Hello? Anybody home?" Elaine says.

Brian opens his eyes, and smiles briefly. "Yeah," he says, somewhat guiltily, and regrets even thinking about guilt. Elaine stands at his left, and the door opens to admit the dentist, a medium tall man in typical white buttoned smock with complimentary pocket protector. Dr. Michaels, Brian knows, will stick several large needles' worth of novacaine into his cheeks. Brian prepares to close his eyes.

"Well, Brian," Dr. Michaels says, extending a hand to shake. "We all set? Good," he says, Brian nodding, "well, let's get you all good and numbed up."

The dentist crosses to the sink, washes thoroughly, Elaine doing something not quite into Brian's line of vision. Brian remains calm as possible, waiting patiently. Dr. Michaels reaches for the first of the needles, and Brian instantly shuts his eyes and opens his mouth.

"All right, Brian, here we go..."

Pinpricks in each cheek, two or three in each, Brian can't tell. He squirms a bit as the icy cold fluid infects warm, red tissue like a plague. Dr. Michaels is gone. Elaine stays behind rearranging items on a metal tray against the left-hand wall, drawing back a blue cloth and replacing it two or three times.

Brian withdraws into himself, searching, searching. Time passes. His eyes open and Elaine stands over him. The metal tray stand hovers above his waist, just out of reach.

"All right, Brian?" she says. Her eyes appear to smile, but Brian can't tell because of the white mask she wears strapped on by strings around her ears.

"Yes," he says slowly. The numbness is setting in, he knows, and soon he will be unable to say anything intelligible. He nods and says again, "Yes. Can't talk."

Now he is certain she smiles. "Yeah, feels weird, doesn't it?"

Brian nods, and verges on closing his eyes as she continues.

"Looks like it'll snow this weekend," she says, clasping her hands in front of her on the metal tray. She looks off into the distance, stage right. "Already getting cold."

Brian attempts another smile, feeling a strange resistance to the tugging at the corners of his mouth. "Okay," he utters eventually, "like snow."

"You from around here?" Elaine says, turning her eyes back to him. "I'm from Washington State, originally."

He considers. This could turn out to be a rather awkward conversation, he thinks. Again the tug of war with his own facial muscles, resulting in, "Up Pen...insa."

"You're from the Upper Peninsula?" she says, her voice raising at the end of her statement. He knows now, does Brian, had she not told him where in the world she was from, he would know she was not from Michigan. It's U. P., he thinks. You pee, not Upper Peninsula. Just the initials.

"Yah," he says thickly, resisting the urge to lift a hand to his rapidly freezing mouth. His lips feel swollen, grown together into a shapeless formless mass. He tries to think of an appropriate metaphor for what is happening to him, but fails. Sensation has been slowly fleeing his face, and he is not even aware of it.

"My cousin's from northern Michigan," the nurse says. She toys with the instruments on the metal tray with her gloved hands. Brian watches with a detached expression; it is the only expression he feels he can manage, not knowing what his face will resemble if he tries anything else. She sighs softly, letting her hands lay on the tray amongst the cutlery. "He lives in Detroit now, but he goes out of his way to let people know he's from the country. He hates the city."

Brian notices she also pronounces that name incorrectly. It's Dee-troit. Deeee-troit. He debates asking where in Michigan her cousin is from, ponders raising his hand with the fingers together, "the mitten" shape of Michigan, then pointing to where Ann Arbor roughly is. But he decides against it. Brian's mother lives in Pennsylvania now, for the past decade lives there, and already she forgets the mitten. Last time Brian talked to his mother, she kept asking him if he were surrounded by militiamen. Even when he told her, "No, Mom, they're up near Flint," the reassurance that Brian's city is more than a three-hour drive from anyone with a basement full of fertilizer is not much reassurance to a mother.

Brian glances at the tiny window to the outside world. Leaves stubbornly cling to trees, but soon he knows the winds will pick up and his business will drop off as pedestrians stay indoors.

"Do you go to the university?" Elaine's voice says.

Brian tries to open his mouth, "Uhh..." *What should I say?* he wonders, then abruptly decides that lying to a person he most likely will never see again his entire life doesn't really count as a lie. "Uh...graduated last year...I write..."

The last part of the lie is actually a semi-truth, as most lies tend to go. He does write occasionally, with a friend of his drawing and inking the issues. Nothing big, nothing spectacular, and certainly nothing satanic, no matter what various parents would say about Brian's studies, no matter what Elaine might say if he tells her the entire truth. None of his Tarot card interpretations or Carl Jung references or Israel Regardie books have the slightest thing in common with satanic cults. His 10,000 Buddhist prostrations every two months have nothing to do with anything, and everything to do with nothing. Brian smiles at the thought. *I love contradictions, they make life bearable.* He wonders how long it's been since he said something. He wonders if he actually can smile or if his brain is simply being fooled.

"Uh...children's books..." he blurts. His tongue lolls back and forth. "Sorry..." he adds slowly, "...can't talk too well..."

Elaine nods, giving no indication of how long she may be waiting for her responses. "That's okay. Starting to feel pretty numb?"

Brian nods, aware that the mass of hair behind his head is becoming slightly uncomfortable. He squirms a bit in the chair, Elaine moves behind the chair and attempts to adjust the headrest for him, to some relief. He relaxes again, deliberately relaxes his shoulders, arms, thighs, calves. The dentist may arrive soon, however soon soon may be. Elaine places a heavy, metallic phallus shaped object on the triangular portion of Brian's abdomen, between his navel and his crotch, a cord dangling off one end, and then closes the door behind her.

Brian rolls his eyes downward as far as they can go, but does not move his head. Laying perpendicular to Brian's line of vision on a cloth of white, the drill slowly shudders up and down in perfect rhythm with Brian's pulse.

He had to get up out of the chair and walk down the hallway to the X-ray room. Brian grunted resignedly as Elaine helped him to his feet, and shook his head groggily.

"Feeling kinda out of it, huh?" she said sympathetically.

He nodded and hesitantly touched fingertips to his cheeks. They were icy cold, completely numb to the touch. If he hadn't watched his fingers rise to his face, he wouldn't have known his face was still there. Where his lips should have been there was only a formless blob of flesh, disembodied and floating a few feet away from the bone. Brian tried to smile, and then touched his mouth to determine how it had reacted. The corners of his mouth had slightly lifted in response, but the rest had stayed limp. Well, he thought, at least I can sort of half-smile.

"Sorry to have to do this to you," Elaine said as she directed Brian into a chair in the x-ray room and closed the door behind. "I know it's kind of a pain, but we need to make sure we got all the root tips out. If we miss any, it's going to mean you'll have to come back again anyway, and I'm sure you don't want to have to do that."

Brian grimaced, and this time he was pretty sure he actually did grimace. He touched his lips lightly. Yes, he had. He folded his arms as Elaine laid a large, heavy lead jacket across his entire body, from neck to ankle. She then maneuvered a robotic arm with a cylinder at the end and pointed it at Brian's right cheek.

*Oh, no,* he thought, realizing what was to come next.

His jaws pried open, Brian felt the cardboard taste of the one by two inch rectangle shoved between his teeth and cheek. Back, back, back some more it went, until he felt himself begin to gag.

"Hnnh!" he said painfully, eyes darting. At the corner of his right eye Brian could see another nurse, an unfamiliar woman, jiggling a plastic arm of some sort with the x-ray rectangle attached to the end which banged against his teeth and rubbed against his numb mouth.

"Sorry," she said, trying to sound apologetic and not quite succeeding. She pulled the X-ray strip out and readjusted it at the end of the arm before prying jaws open again and reshoving it. "It's got to get back there," she explained to his further gagging noises. "It's real far back there."

The cardboard taste was overwhelming. Brian felt tears forming in the corners of his eyes and viciously suppressed them. His tongue flopped on over to the rectangular strip out of curiosity and quickly fled. "Bite down, please," the nurse instructed. He did, and the strip tilted into his upper gum, biting into the flesh connecting gum to cheek. A muscle near his nose bridge twinged. Brian gasped and opened his jaws again, letting the plastic arm sticking out of his mouth to rattle before he clamped down again. The nurse grumped, grasping the plastic arm and making further readjustments.

After a few moments, the nurse deemed all was in order. Positioning the open-ended cylinder end of the swiveling robotic arm up against the back corner of the right side of Brian's face, she disappeared behind a wall to the left. Brian heard a clicking electrical noise inside his head, and the nurse was then withdrawing the one by two inch moistened white cardboard rectangle from his mouth. Brian stood carefully, removing the lead vest, and Elaine reappeared to help him back down the hallway. Once in the first dentist's chair, Brian sighed and lay back into his hair again, closing his eyes as they waited for the X-ray results.

He had to go back and have another x-ray. The first one hadn't been back far enough in the mouth.

A song is what he hears. He cannot feel his face; that's the point, he knows, vaguely now, that if he could feel his face he probably would be screaming in utter agony. Underneath the steady light and underneath the quiet grating top 40 music, Brian hears a memory.

It's a mask, he thinks, desperately slipping into the past, glancing about for movie highlights. A thick, damp, heavy mask paralyzing him. A shadow which somehow fell across the lower half of his face and left his hearing intact, left him aware of his surroundings but unable or unwilling to affect them. He knows he has a choice. He could, he knows, at any moment sit upright with a start and bolt out the door, blood streaming in rainbow ribbons from the corners of his mouth, strip-striping his black beard, but this he would not do.

The song comes back in now stronger, and Brian begins to think he recognizes it finally. Its name is One, and Brian remembers that he used to like this band before he joined the Buddhist Dharma center. To be sure, he still listens occasionally to the older bands such as Black Sabbath, from way back, but only if a fellow worker happens to throw a tape in the deck. He never listens to that now. It's in the past, but the song grows stronger still, begins pounding at the base of his neck.Brian images the video in his mind...

*I don't know whether I'm alive and dreaming or...*

113

Experimentally Brian attempts to flop his tongue about. A strong metallic prod stops the motion, and there is a sucking sensation, as if through a tiny tube, jammed between his lower jaw and his cheek. At least what he thinks is the cheek. He can't feel that, either, and this unnerves him. He knows what will happen. Occasionally, Brian senses liquid slowly filling up the space between teeth and cheek, before it slowly is sucked away, but he cannot feel his face.

*Inside me I'm screaming...*

Eyelids flutter but they do not open. Oh God, he thinks, what is going on. What am I doing, what is being done? His fingers clench tighter now, pulling away from each other yet towards. A slight whining noise fills his skull, starting at the lower left corner of his mouth and crawling quickly up behind his right ear and over his eyebrows.

*I'm just like a piece of meat...*

The metal song riveting his divided attention, Kirk Hammet's V-shaped Strat jackhammers thirty-second notes into his molars, bouncing around his incisors and piercing up into his palate. Words scream into his sinus cavities, and Brian, working himself down from a panic, tries not to think of Dalton Trumbo.

*...that keeps on living....*

*Oh, god,* Brian thinks. *Oh, god, I can't stand yogurt.*

"Just a little noise," sang the dentist.

"A little noise," sang the nurse.

Brian just then felt pressure tighten around his upper left jaw, millimeters from the joining of the jaws. The report of a crackling snap reverberated throughout his skull.

Brian remembers when he used to know some Latin. Indeed, he realizes that if he knew more Latin it would help his occult studies into the mystic realms of Henry Cornelius Agrippa and Hermes Trismegistus, Pliny (the older one) and Erasmus. The only thing he could recall from his brief stab at Classical Latin were the various cases; nominative, accusative, genitive, dative...it was instrumental he was reminded of for some reason, the case which demonstrated how or with what something was used, as in: "Jane kicked John with her leg."

Suddenly, of its own volition, and without any prior notification whatsoever, Brian's right leg chose that moment to go instrumental on the chair.

"Mmmmpfff!" Brian said.

The dentist must have let go, but the pain shot heedlessly upwards and outwards in pulsating power surges as Brian forced his eyes open. Nasty vile thoughts swirled around Brian's steel-toe booted foot as his knee flexed and relaxed.

"Now, Brian, if you feel pain, you have to let me know, okay?" the dentist admonished, backing away from Brian with his body but not with his face.

*You stupid shit!* Brian thought. *How the hell am I supposed to tell you anything when you have your fingers shoved down my throat?*

"Mm-MM-pffmm!" he said.

The dentist frowned slightly behind his thin glasses and motioned to the nurse. He said down to Brian, "Do you think you need it to be numbed again? It's up to you, you know."

"MmmpffFFpp."

Brian tried to glare and wince at the same time and wound up shutting his eyes tight instead and curling his toes. He felt the hard plastic square wedge higher up his right jaw, his mouth prying apart as the dentist said, "Clamp down on that, for leverage, there you go."

The wedge dug into the upper and lower gums. Brian began to wonder what exactly it might look like back there, with the wedge bloodying itself, taking the place of two teeth which until recently had rested within soft yet hard orange-red tissue, minding their own business until a higher power decided it better to untimely rip them from their sockets.

The thought disappeared as a dagger sharply pierced his upper left jaw and neatly sliced his left eyeball from his cheekbone.

"Aaaa," was all he could manage.

Another piercing jab shot straight upwards, encasing his forehead in mute nostril agony. The cracking noise echoed from ear to ear.

"Aa-aaAAaa," he said again. Images of applesauce and milk shakes filled the dark spaces which swam where his eyes should have been. Cool liquid splashed around his mouth, and he involuntarily swallowed.

"There we are," Dr. Michaels' voice said softly. The plastic square wedged in Brian's face released itself from his bloody sockets, and he sighed in ecstasy from the pain.

"What if God were one of us..." the dentist mumbled to the ceiling sounds.

Brian sensed motion from the dentist, thinking that perhaps Dr. Michaels had removed himself to the counter top. His hands stopped fidgeting a while ago, but Brian still couldn't bring himself to open his eyes. A set of hands opened his mouth again and tilted his head back.

"Okay, Brian," the dentist said, "what we're going to do now is put in some sutures to help the healing process."

Brian felt a tug in his lower right gum, then a strange stringy taste as the thread rubbed against the corner of his mouth. The scissoring action of Dr. Michaels bounced down the thread into Brian's teeth.

"Now, these sutures are dissolvable, so you shouldn't have to come back," Dr. Michaels continued in a calm, sing-song voice. "But, if you need to come back, or if you have any problems at all, just give us a call, okay?"

He finished with the bottom right suture and began to work on the upper. "Now, what I'm going to do is give you a prescription for painkillers. Tylenol-3 is a codeine/narcotic analgesic. And you'll also be taking decadron pills, to keep the swelling down, okay? I'll write those out for when we get done here."

Brian felt another snip, and another. *Hormone pills*, he thought distantly. *They mess you up.* The thread rubbed into the left corner of his mouth, then a hand shoved sizeable cottony-tasting wads into his cheeks.

"All done now," Dr. Michaels said. Brian opened his eyes. The dentist shook Brian's hand. "Well, there you are. Elaine will give you a list of directions concerning proper dental care during the first few days or so, all right? You just give us a call if you need anything else." The dentist nodded seriously, then smiled and turned and left the room.

Elaine quickly wiped the blood from Brian's beard.

## Ode to Shelley

And when all is said and done,
far from now when I am gone
will I exist as no more than a name—
will these tiny scratchings alone spell out the
entirety of my life, to reconstruct the
minutes and seconds of what it meant
to be alive, to be human, to be me.

For I will have no mighty works to
look upon and despair,
I will have no glorious battles and
fame to write into history;
there will be no foundations, no statues,
no roads, no towns, no family to bear my name,
much less myself.

All that will be left are the words,
the letters. The syllables.
Sounds of creation and memory,
locking up the intangible for a short, brief moment—

...but even these fade, even these are merely
mortal. Who will wonder
what manner of proud beast once
crouched in this place—
fearful of oblivion, hopeful all the same.

## The Green and the Grey

I boarded the Greyhound at mid-afternoon. The Albany station was packed, as usual. Students crowded around the ticket windows in a confused and confusing shuffling mob, men in staid grey suits ignored the women with noisy children and read their folded copies of the New York Times, announcements barked throughout the terminal over unseen speakers. I hugged my shoulder bag as the people squirmed down the center aisle. An elderly woman in a brown coat, a faded red scarf for a bonnet, sat in the front seat directly behind the driver. A heavy-set man with white sideburns lay back on the opposite front seat, draped his hand over the padded metal railing. Left alone in my pair of seats, I placed my bag next to me and began reading a book. The driver came up the three steps, glanced around his bus, and sat down with a grunt. He gunned the engine, let it set to warm up as he rifled through a clipboard of paperwork. I adjusted my chair back the maximum allowance of three inches and sighed.

The driver cleared his throat over the intercom. "Please make sure all your baggage is secured below or in the storage racks above your seats. This is a non-smoking coach." The bus slipped into gear and lurched forward before catching itself, rumbling into the right-hand lane. The driver coaxed the bus into silence as we passed the New York State Capitol Building to the left and looked down from the top of overlapping highway ramps at the Hudson River on the right. A few minutes to reach the Thruway exit and to collect the ticket and we were on our way, southward bound.

The on-ramp opened out into two lanes of slate-grey concrete, cracked from age and disrepair, bordered by green and brown grass and stunted trees. I gazed through the window at the city dwindling into the countryside hills, and fingered the pages of my book. The bus hummed.

"They say it's going to snow," said the woman in the front.

"Um-hmm," responded the driver, without turning his head.

The woman was silent for a moment. "It'll be the first snowfall of the year," she said finally. "Might get up to a foot."

"Maybe sixteen inches, even," said the man across the aisle in a deep voice.

"Um-hmm," the driver said.

"It's real nasty, driving in weather like that," the woman persisted. "The roads'll get all iced up, then covered with snow, and then iced again, and you can't see through the snow to begin with..." Pause. The flat hiss of the heater vainly trying to keep us warm.

"Be hard to get anywheres," she concluded, wiping her nose.

"Yes'm," the driver said, keeping his eyes to the road, "I do believe it's started already."

The woman sat up and leaned forward. "Why, it sure has." She sighed and sat down again. "I hope this winter isn't as bad as last year. I don't know if we could take it. Heating bills and all that. It's starting to cost us, getting up there."

The man in the front seat grunted and shifted his weight.

"Last winter was kind of strange," she continued, not taking notice of the man across from her. "It'd be warm for a couple of days, like in the 40s, then freezing the next week. It'd snow, then be clear, then sleet, then rain...all sorts of nasty stuff. You never knew what was going to happen next."

"Yes'm," the driver said. "That was one mighty strange winter."

"But I guess you just have to live with it," she said. The other two nodded, but she didn't notice. "You just got to make the best of it, do what you got to do, and keep on living."

She sat back, looking out the window as flecks of snow came down, the movement of the bus transforming them into streams of white thread. The bus was silent for a little while. A girl behind got up to go to the bathroom stall in the back. The CB up front crackled, faint voices heard discussing the weather report. The driver picked up his mike and talked softly into it.

"How long you been doing this?" the woman asked suddenly.

"Me? I don't know, 'bout ten, fifteen years," the driver responded.

"You know who Henry is? You know, old Henry with the wooden foot?"

"Yeah, I think I know who you're talking about. I picked him up a couple of times. He always wanted to be dropped off the side of the road outside Albany."

"That's Henry," the woman laughed. The laugh sounded shrill in the silence. People in the back looked up to see what was the matter. "Henry used to live in a little house right off old Route 9. He built it with his own two hands, lived by himself. He'd come into town once in a while, but he never stayed long. Must have been lonely out there."

"He talked a good game," said the driver. "Nice guy, told some pretty funny stories."

"Yeah, Henry was a great guy. He wouldn't accept charity. We tried to give him food, money...he didn't want it. Said he could manage on his own." The woman sighed. "I wonder whatever happened to him."

"Haven't seen him in, oh, must be a couple of years," said the driver.

"It's too bad people have to live like that," the woman said. "People like Henry, they need some help from folks who are better off. They work hard their whole lives, and at the end they deserve a little respect. It's hard, living."

The man opposite her grunted again. "Hard to make a living," he grumbled. "Work day in, day out, try to save a little for later, and pray to God you make it. That's what life's about."

The woman laughed. "I try telling my granddaughter that," she said. "She's in college now, eighteen years old. She won't listen to me. Thinks I'm too 'old-fashioned,' I don't know what I'm talking about." She sighed, tugging her scarf tighter under her skin. "Kids. Can't tell 'em anything. She'll learn soon enough, though, when she goes to get a job. She'll have to learn the hard way, I guess."

"Only way to learn," the man said.

"My youngest son's going to Albany," the driver said. "SUNY Albany. I'm putting him through myself. He thinks he's there just to play basketball, but I make sure he gets good grades. He's taking business. I want him to have a good job."

The woman and the man said nothing.

"I figure I got about eight more years before I retire," the driver said. "Maybe I'll spend some time home, maybe I'll go fishing some, see a couple of ball games. Teach my grandkids how to play football."

The driver turned on the lights and the wipers. The engine whined as he eased up on the accelerator. "I'm retired now," said the woman. "I used to work for the State. Fifteen years in a tollbooth. Before that, it was another fifteen years behind a switchboard."

"You worked for the State?" the driver asked.

"Fifteen years," the woman said. "I stood fifteen years in a little box at exit 24. I got cold and tired, so I retired after fifteen years. I had enough." She chuckled. "Now, I had enough of retirement. I got to find something to do."

"I was in the Army for twenty years," said the man. "Didn't do me much good, but it gave me something to do. Wasn't a bad job. But I got out when I heard about this Somalia thing. I had enough of that."

"It's a shame about that. People starving so we got to send in our boys to clean it up. I don't understand why we got to do it, but I guess we're the best, so we just do the best and then get out. And what's that other place, Yugoslavia? Didn't they have the Olympics there a while back?"

"Uh huh," said the driver. "In '84."

"Seems like people been fighting each other over there forever," the woman said. "People shooting each other, and bombing churches, killing kids and babies..." she shivered. "It makes you wonder."

"Sure does," said the driver.

"All this fighting and wars going on," the woman continued. "Makes you wonder how people have made it this far. Everywhere around the world people are dying and killing each other, and there's famines and diseases and such. It's a hard world, a rough world out there. Sometimes we don't realize how lucky we are."

"Sure could be worse," the driver said.

"You just got to look around," said the woman, sweeping her hand toward the windows. "Look around at all the trees and the hills and the grass and the sky. Just look at the beauty of nature, and you know that there just has to be a reason. You just got to thank God for all this beauty, and you got to thank God that we can be a part of it."

"Yeah," said the driver.

"You just got to," repeated the woman, and lapsed into silence.

I put on my headphones, listening to an obscure Scottish band, and looked out at the Hudson Valley and the greying sky. The snow was falling harder now, dropping a thin wet blanket over the hills and shrubs along the highway. The bus's wipers whisked across the glass, opening arced eyes to the flurry. If I looked just at the right angle, I could see my reflection in the side window, looking out, looking in.

The bus shuddered and slowed as we approached the exit at Kingston. We glided over the encrusted roadway to the tollbooth, pausing momentarily to pay, passing into the traffic circle beyond. The first right led us to the station. The bus slowly rolled to a halt, wheels locking, packing the snow on the ground with a crunch. The driver dictated bus transfer information over the intercom in a matter-of-fact, offhand manner. "Please take all your personal belongings with you. Thank you for riding Greyhound, and have a happy holiday." He got up and left the bus. The woman followed with her scarfed head down. The sideburned man stayed in his seat staring straight ahead while others shuffled past.

I retrieved my suitcase from the storage compartments below and walked to the adjacent dimly-lit parking lot. Where a week ago there were dirty streets and sooty sandstone buildings all was now white. No car horns, no wheels spinning. No footsteps. The snowflakes drifting down and sparkling in the overhead parking lights.

I spotted their blue wagon covered with snow in a far corner of the lot. From their car, finally, two rapidly filling trails of footprints. They led me to a nearby diner. I pushed the door open and drank in the warm air, slung my bag over my shoulder and dragged my suitcase between the booths to the back. Two familiar, friendly faces stopped mid-conversation and smiled in greeting as I dropped my bag to the floor.

"Hi," I said, leaning over the booth with a smile. "Ready to go?"

## Asian Dreams

After this night you will be a memory—less,
not even a person.
I will have no recollection of you at all.

You have no substance you are only form. You
subscribe to order,
you pray to the great paper green god. You
supplicate generations to the
cross-eyed self-alienating beast of the Mideast rising.

You have no power over me any more.

I do not bear the claddagh, I do not sport the gold,
the marked silver which dully shines,
hanging from threads from chains.
Unwanted reminder, insistent remembrance, of
where I once was, who I
once was, and occasionally still am,
despite.

Tonight I will dream Asian dreams of selflessness,
doubtless but worrisome—
the sacrifice of I, hanging myself for my own sake,
unworthy of demons or angels, two enemies to keep at
bay from
the complacency of self.

Once again listening to the songs I couldn't bring myself
to hear
after her

after one night
satin silk red sheets and long caresses, we thought it
beautifully ironic,
mischievous to make love to
His music. A Mid-eastern romance.

How long ago it seems!
Yesterday really is the same as
today and tomorrow.

The trickling roadside ditch water out my window
will always be there, and
will never be there, and
will always have been there,
in some form or other.
Perhaps so have I.

We are all fools of different natures—
you, and I, and the water.

## Training the Mountain Warrior

So there I was, deliberately dangling my friend off a mountain cliff in central Japan.

Believe me, this wasn't in our original plan, but that's how things wound up in the end. Just goes to show… something, I suppose. About choices and happenstance.

Ben K and I were both teaching English on the Japan Exchange Teacher program at the time. I say "teaching" although more often than not it seemed that we were in the classrooms of Japanese students just to provide a bit of comic relief from their excruciatingly boring grammar lessons.

Ben had come over a year before I did. Originally from the Chicago area, he called LA home and was outgoing, friendly...blond...everything I was not. He was the kind of person that would walk up to a total stranger, grab his hand, and say, "Hey, how's it going?" as if he had known the guy his entire life. A naturally suspicious New Yorker, I was the opposite. Even though I lived in a town only a short drive from his, I hadn't thought to introduce myself for the first eight or nine months after my arrival.

I touched down at Narita Airport, just outside Tokyo, on July 28, 1999. Three days later, I traveled by bullet train with the other new 40-some-odd native speakers of English who would be new assistant language teachers in Nara Prefecture, the ancient capital. On the first day of my life in Nara, at a one-day orientation of sort, I received a telephone list with photos of all the prefectural assistant language teachers. That's when I found out that they, not I, would be in the ancient capital. I was posted to a small "designated city." The semi-rural city was on the last train stop in the prefecture, beyond which lay the Kinai Mountains and several isolated small villages. There were three other non-Japanese in the city, none of whom I knew. At the time, I had no idea how to read Chinese characters or speak Japanese.

My new Japanese high school colleagues dropped me off at the teachers' dormitory where I was to be the sole resident, told me I didn't have any classes until September, and then left. During the month of August I had little to do but get accustomed to not understanding a word anybody said while figuring out how to buy groceries and do my laundry. Resting in the dorm room between occasional day trips to various temples and shrines in the area, I would occasionally take out the telephone list and stare at the photos, wondering what kind of person he or she was. During the orientation, I had only met a handful of the 80 or so faces in the book. I just couldn't bring myself to contact somebody I didn't know.

Over half a year later, on a weekend day in February or March, he called me up suddenly. "Hey, it's Ben, your neighbor. How come you never called me, man? What's up?"

"Uh…"

Ben just kept talking right over me as I basically did nothing but nod at the phone while grunting, "Nn." (a habit that all non-Japanese pick up after living in Japan for a while). It turned out that he had been there for about a year and a half, living in the small village of Tenkawa deep in the mountains south of where I was.

"So," he said at some point. "When are you coming over?"

"Coming over? Where?"

"Here, ya nimrod. I'm only down the road an hour, 45 minutes maybe."

"Dude, I don't have a car. I can't even drive in this country legally."

"Oh. Well, my school gave me a car to use. I'll come pick you up."

And thereafter we started hanging out on a more or less regular basis. Skip forward a month or so to spring and we're walking around downtown Osaka, Ben having left his car at my teacher's dormitory so we could use the nearby JR train.

"Matt, I gotta ask you a serious question," he said, as we were wandering around the Namba shopping area, dodging teenagers on bicycles and older folks on motorized four-wheeler carts. We had stopped in the biggest bookstore in the area, Junkudo, then grabbed some lunch from a ramen place nearby and were now headed for Round One bowling and batting cages.

"OK, shoot."

"How." He paused. "OK, let's say you got this girlfriend you really like."

I nodded and swallowed a sigh. I hadn't dated in years.

"How do you tell her that you really have feelings toward her and, you know..."

He stopped in the middle of the street and grimaced. Gestured with a hand as if about to conduct his own speech at a concert.

"I mean," he began again. We continued walking towards bowling. "OK, look, we're not going to be here forever, you know, in Japan. I'm just starting my last year in JET and after that, I just don't know."

This part of the conversation, I understood. Like all the other teachers in our program, we were placed in elementary, junior or senior high schools for a year at a time, annual contracts renewable twice maximum. I hadn't planned to stay longer than two years, and neither had he. So why was he still in the country? I wondered. So I asked him.

Ben waved a hand in front of his face. "You know why I'm here in the first place, right. There was this girl I was dating in college."

I sighed.

"All right, so I was foolish, following her here. We broke up after I was in the country a couple months. But there was this other girl I had met in Cali."

"Your girlfriend?"

"Yeah, now. But at the time, she went back and we just kind of wrote back and forth. You know, pen pals. Man, that sounds so gay."

I winced. "Dude."

A wave of the hand again. "Yeah, yeah, unPC, I know. Right, anyways."

We were at Round One by now. There was a break in the conversation as we got shoes, paid for a lane, bowled a couple frames while drinking Asahi Super Dry and generally behaving like old college buddies on a night on the town.

Fast-forward another few months, to the end of July, 2001. I had just returned from a family funeral in the US when Ben called me up. "Are you free? Tomorrow?"

"Yeah. Osaka?"

"No. How about Fuji-san?"

"What? Mount Fuji? Now?"

"Yeah. Why not?"

And so we took an overnight bus from Osaka Station to a "station" about halfway up Mt. Fuji. Fuji is a "sunrise" mountain, so that means an overnight stay on the volcano. If you want to see the sunrise, that is. It turned out that Ben's girlfriend Atsuko had helped him arrange for a "package plan," which included the bus fare as well as a one-night stay in what was described to us to as "lodge." We were warned ahead of time to bring raingear and a backpack, as well as a plastic bag or two for garbage. It also turned out that using the toilets on the mountain required a "donation" of about 100 yen each time. The

100-yen coin was supposed to be dropped into a small wooden box next to each tiny toilet stall. I never saw anybody actually pay, though.

After a couple of hours of steady walking through a barren volcanic landscape of black stones and rope handholds, our group was led to the "lodge." It turned out that the style of sleeping was *zakone*—sardine-style, with your head next to somebody else's feet, stacked like tiny fish in a can. The roof was barely high enough to not-quite kneel, and the stench was fairly unbearable. When we first stuck our heads into the low-slung wooden shack and realized what was expected, all I could say, repeatedly, was "You gotta be kidding me."

Ben just started laughing. After a while, lying there with my nose literally inches from a stranger's smelly wool socks, I started laughing, too.

"I can't wait to tell Atsuko about this," Ben giggled from near my feet.

"You think she knew?" I asked.

"Probably. Getcher damn feet out of my face."

"Go screw."

I spent the next half hour trying to get Ben to properly pronounce "fugeddaboutit," and he reciprocated by unsuccessfully training me to sound like Al Capone.

I doubt we slept even a minute of the two and a half hours in the building.

At some point after midnight, we were wakened and the troupe set off up the mountain. It was bitterly cold, and after a half hour the rain started. I honestly don't recall how long we trudged that night/morning, one foot in front of the other, only pausing to shout, "This sucks" at each other, as we all desperately tried to continue climbing Fuji in the dark. Up ahead, we could see what appeared to be headlights from towers marking the mountain's summit.

The wind picked up and whipped around us. The leaders of the travel group scurried back and forth a few times, arresting our forward movement from time to time. Eventually, as we were about to make the final ascent, they stopped us for good. It was too windy to reach the top. We had been ordered to go back for safety reasons, a mere hundred meters from the goal.

Another hour of retracing our steps, and we rested at a ledge overlooking a lush green valley. The sun slowly appeared above the horizon as the rain subsided, and fellow hikers took out their cameras to snap a few shots. We were so annoyed that we didn't even bother.

"Man, this has got to be the most miserable night of my life," Ben said, shaking his head. "Incredibly frustrating."

I could only agree. "You wanna try this again?" Mt Fuji is only open in the summer months, and since this was the start of his final year, we would only have one more chance.

"Nah," he said. "You know the saying? A wise man climbs Fuji once, a fool goes twice."

It was then that I ventured to ask about his future plans. He and I had barely talked about Atsuko in the preceding few months since he raised the issue.

"You know," he said, removing his poncho and rolling it up, "I just don't know. Haven't really got any plans yet."

"This is beginning of your last year in JET, right?"

"Yeah, it's just." He shoved the roll of plastic into his pack and hoisted it up as we started back down again, to the bus that would take us back to Osaka.

"Just?"

He pursed his lips in thought before continuing. "What about you? Are you going to renew for a third year, like me?"

"I dunno," I responded, a bit taken aback. "Hadn't really thought about it yet."

"See?"

"But you're in the third year already. And you got a girlfriend."

"Honestly, Matt, what am I gonna do in California? Go back to LA? For what? I don't even have a teaching license. What can I do?"

"So, you'll stay here, get a job in Osaka?"

"I dunno. The grass is always greener, I guess, huh."

And we let the matter hang. The long night's moroseful march up Fuji-san had exhausted us. What seemed a golden opportunity, almost once-in-a-lifetime, had eluded us. I had already planned a trip back to New York in August to stay with my family for three weeks, and Ben had likewise, though he now had decided to visit with his girlfriend and introduce her to family. It seemed a sign to me, but Ben didn't want to discuss it.

From September, the fall months were a blur of school-related teaching activities. Ben and I hung out a few times in October and November, but always in Osaka, always in the city, where we could go bowling, or play pool, and of course drink like fish. In the meantime, I had joined a martial arts group and started a weekly running regimen to get my paunch into shape. After New Year's, I didn't hear from Ben. I supposed that he was concentrating on his future. Or his girlfriend. Or both. I focused on my job and my struggles to learn Japanese. Time slipped by.

July arrived again, much too soon. Near the end of the month, about a week after the spring semester had ended, Ben called me finally.

"Hey, what up, bro."

"What's happening? Haven't heard from you in a while. You leaving soon?"

"Yeah, this weekend."

So sudden.

"All right, so what's the plan?"

Pause on the other end of the line. "I gotta talk to you about, you know, stuff."

"Stuff. Like, about Atsuko?"

"Look, Matt, this ain't easy. Whaddya say I stop by and…"

Looking out the balcony doors of my apartment, gazing across the valley to the southern Kinai mountains, I had a vision. "How about we go hiking?"

"It's too late for Fuji-san."

"No, not Fuji. O-mine-san. Let's do the *yamabushi* thing."

Already twice since coming to Japan, I had joined students for a required winter mountain hike up the nearby low-slung Mount Congo, which lay a short walking distance north of the school. Part of a long mountain chain stretching along the Nara-Osaka border, Congo-san was popular among *yamabushi*, or "mountain warriors." The ascetic practice these mountain warriors practice is called *shugendo*, or "the path of training," and was supposedly founded by a mystical monk named Enno-gyojya in the seventh century. Enno-gyojya was said to have walked up and down mountains three times a day for decades and eventually attained enlightenment simply by walking. All around the region, there were bronze

138

statues of Enno-gyojya, in typical medieval Buddhist monk garb, wearing iron *geta* shoes and holding a *shakujyo* staff topped with metal rings that bang against each other as you walk.

The idea of hiking to enlightenment probably sounds faintly ridiculous until you consider where these hiking paths go. The mountains in the area south of where I was living—literally in Ben's backyard—range from around 5600 to 6300 feet in height and feature steep slopes, pine tree-covered ridges like folded dark green origami. Hiking in these mountains is an imposing experience, especially when you're surrounded by over 500 purple-gym uniform clad students walking up narrow, four-foot dirt trails with banks that disappear into sheer drops of several hundred feet with no handholds or rails. But unlike the short one-day paths used for school trips, the real mountain paths, the ones used by the *yamabushi*, took days to traverse and went deep into the mountains, peppered by the occasional ramshackle *yama-goya* mountain lodge.

Like me, Ben had gone for school excursions into the mountains with students. The schools treated such trips as day-long P.E. classes, but they avoided the more strenuous paths. Also, because the true *yamabushi* paths often forbade women and were associated with esoteric religious practices, the schools were naturally reluctant to go to certain areas.

Not us. We'd only one weekend left and while we'd been into the mountains, we'd never set foot on O-mine-san, the most famous of the lot.

So of course, he said, "OK, sure, hell, why not?"

When Ben pulled his red Honda up to the teacher's dorm and I jumped in, I noticed two things immediately.

The first thing was his right arm in a sling. The second was glasses.

He gestured to the glasses right away with a dismissive wave of a hand. "Yeah, dorky, I know, right?"

I had worn glasses since age 7, but had tried soft contact lenses the previous year. To no avail. Dry eye and an inability to get the damn things out had me back to glasses after only four weeks. I'd had no idea that Ben wore contacts.

"No, man, they look good on you."

"Yeah? No kidding?"

My turn.

"OK, the arm?"

He shrugged, turning the Honda onto the first of many mountain roads to Tenkawa. "Broke my wrist, actually."

"How?"

"I got into a car accident in November."

"Jeez."

"Yeah. I had my arm stuck out the window while I was driving around this, you know, pretty typical mountain road curve, right? You know how these roads are sometimes so narrow that only one car can go and you have to keep looking in these mirrors all the time?"

He said this, gesturing with a nod at the round, orange-fringed mirrors that were located at every single curve in every Japanese road. It was true; when I'd been driven to some junior high schools in these same mountains, the roads were so narrow that occasionally when two cars met coming opposite directions, there was a silent negotiation over which one had to back up for four or five minutes to let the other pass.

I silently prayed to Enno-gyojya as Ben took us around another hairpin turn using his off hand.

"So this other guy was coming towards me pretty fast, and I swerved to avoid him," he continued, yanking the wheel into another turn. "Slammed right into a rock wall and broke it. Banged up the car real good, too. The school wasn't happy about it."

"How bad is it?" I asked, referring to the wrist.

"It's basically back to normal, sort of. Doc says I need to keep the sling on just in case for another week. But the cast is off. I just don't have full motion yet."

"And," he went on, in a lower voice as if someone had bugged the car, "don't tell my school. I was texting Atsuko at the time."

"You what?"

"Yeah," he said, sheepishly. "There was no other driver. It was just me being fucking stupid."

I couldn't help but agree.

"So, are you OK to go hiking?"

"C'mon, Matt," he jerked back in disdain. "My hand hurts, not my leg. I'm good."

We parked at his modern-looking steel and concrete apartment, grabbed our backpacks from the back seat, and headed for the trail entrance. Along the road to the mountain trail, we passed more traditional-looking Japanese country homes: wooden, single-story, tiled roofs with tapered ends sporting *oni* demon faces, or images of the Buddha, or one of the Seven Lucky Gods. Set right up against the road, older houses had virtually no windows; instead, all openings were covered with wood-slat sliding doors, the owner's name chiseled permanently into the door frame.

After almost two kilometers on the single-lane, shoulderless road, we reached the entrance to the mountain trail itself, marked by a single squat wooden post with the carved white Chinese characters *Ideguchi.* Entrance/exit. After a few yards following a gradual inclining slope into the woods, the path forked in front of several wooden signs.

"Which way?" Ben asked.

I looked at the signs and identified our destination: O-miné-san, 2 hours walk. "This way," I pointed.

"Lead on, MacDuff."

In the beginning, the trail was fairly easy, but after about an hour, it quickly began to climb. Rainwater had dug deeply into the trail and often it became little more than a narrow ditch with earthen banks five or six feet high on each side. Thin pine trees densely occupied every square inch of the mountainside, leftovers from the reconstructive years of the "postwar miracle" of Japan. The housing boom of the '50s and '60s inspired companies to plant millions of seedlings, in the hopes of raking in a fortune. But the boom died down, and trees from other countries became cheaper. As a result, the young trees, planted closely together to ensure straight growth, were too expensive to thin out to an appropriate number per area. Many of the trees in this area were roughly the same width as an average roll of paper towels and were easily knocked over by strong storms.

After a half hour or so the path began to undulate, and the terrain became rockier. The artificially-planted trees were replaced by natural growth, rotten logs lying across the path where they fell, moss-covered boulders thrown up by forces unseen causing the path to dip and sway before rising again inexorably. We reached an open spot that looked out over the valley below and stopped to take a breather.

After my aborted hike up Mt. Fuji with Ben the previous summer, I found myself noticing more and more what I should have seen before but perhaps was too confused or disoriented to comprehend. Now, breathing heavily in between sips of cold wheat tea from my silver thermos, I could see a difference in color between those trees planted and never thinned out in the distance, and the indigenous copses closer to where we stood, perched above the gorge. The effect was a shimmering carpet with a soft green sponge-like appearance.

"Fuckin' A," Ben exclaimed philosophically.

A perfect opportunity to ask about his future.

"So, you were texting Atsuko?"

He swigged from his own bottle. "Yeah, we've been seeing each other fairly regularly, you might say. She wanted me to meet her family a couple months ago."

"Sounds serious."

"Yeah, well." He stopped and a slightly embarrassed grin spread across his face.

"What, man. Spill it."

He shrugged again, characteristically, and shook his head. "Nah, this is kind of goofy..."

I insisted.

"All right, I arranged something ahead of time without telling her, in a nice restaurant."

"You proposed?"

"Keep your shorts on, I'm getting to it." He shoved me with a grunt. "I'm pretty sure she knew it was coming, right? So I got a ring, and I gave it one of the waiters and told him to bring it out when I gave him this sign." He gestured.

"OK. And?"

"And, I started telling her about me leaving Japan, and what a difficult decision it was for me to make and all that. And then I made the sign, and the waiter brought out two glasses of champagne, and the ring was in one of them. So I fished it out and got down on one knee, right in the middle of the restaurant and told her that I couldn't go back to America alone and and I wouldn't leave Japan without her."

He turned red and grinned again. "I know, real goofy and romantic, right? The whole restaurant was clapping and taking pictures."

"So she said yes?"

He snorted. "Well, jeez, what else is she gonna say at that point? In a way, it was kind of sneaky and unfair of me to do that to her. But I think she was happy. Anyway, she cried."

"Man," what was I going to say? "Uh, congratulations, bro! Man, though, you are a piece of work."

"Yeah, I'm a real stinker, ain't I?"

We shouldered our packs again and got back on the path. As we climbed further, we could see the ravages of the vicious typhoon of 1998, which had knocked down vast swathes of trees like bowling pins or dominos. Trees remained piled one up on top of the other, untouched at the bottom of gullies here and there. Soon we found ourselves face to face with a wooden gate, and a sign proclaiming, "No admittance to women."

"Good thing Atsuko isn't here," Ben commented. But we had both known about this restriction. It meant that we were nearing the temple itself.

The final approach took us past stone lanterns and stele on both sides of an increasingly steep path, past a shed similar in size to the one we had used at Mt. Fuji but coated in corrugated aluminum like many older houses down in the valley. It was just past this point that we met an older Japanese man dressed not in the white of the yamabushi but in regular worker's overalls.

"[Konnichi wa] Good afternoon," we said to him, and bowed.

He stopped in surprise. "Why are you here?"

We looked at each other. Why *were* we here?

"To climb O-miné-san, of course," Ben replied, in all seriousness.

"You speak Japanese well," the man commented. "Where are you from? Are you English teachers?"

Since his spoken Japanese was better than mine, I let Ben do the talking. "We're both American, and yes, we're teachers. I'm leaving soon, though, and my friend here will be in Japan another year."

"Oh, you're leaving? There aren't many tourists on the weekdays from this direction. Let me show you."

Ben turned to me. "Matt, did he just offer to guide us?" he asked me in English.

I shrugged. "Sounds like it."

Mr. Yamamoto (as it turned out) led us without hesitation to a sheer rock face that went straight up at a near 180 degree angle. There were simple ropes and chains attached to the rock with metal hooks. He gestured.

Ben gaped. "This way?"

A nod.

"Just go," I urged.

"Matt, I can't use my right hand."

"I'll go first and help you up."

Up we went, across a rock ridge with quite literally nothing on the side. What few trees there were seemed to be growing from the rocks themselves, roots emerging from within the crevices. We struggled upwards without speaking, Mr. Yamamoto behind us silently.

At some point, what was left of the path opened up onto a bowl-shaped area, with a rock wall going up on the left and two or three largish boulders on the right. A length of twisted rope the width of my forearm lay curled around a single iron peg hammered into the rock wall.

"What a view!" Ben practically shouted, nearly out of breath as he was.

I stared. The panorama was unworldly. Birds flew beneath us, chirruping and warbling across the open space. The deep mountains near the horizon had a fringe of snow on their tops. A cloud-wisped skyline, a patch of terraced rice fields in near distance, in the far distance major road construction towers for a highway that would soon cleave the mountains. There was nothing we couldn't see.

Yamamoto-san gestured again. "Do you want to confess?"

"Confess?" Ben repeated.

I didn't understand the word at first, but the gesture at the rope carried an obvious meaning.

Ben and I exchanged glances, and as if reading my mind, Ben nodded slowly and seriously. "Hey, I'm leaving. When's the next chance?"

He turned to Yamamoto-san and said, "[Yarimashou!] Let's do it!"

Yamamoto-san grunted his assent and began to tie one end of the rope around Ben's shoulders and waist, then wrapped the middle length of the rope around himself, and instructed me to do the same with the rest of the rope. Ben handed me his glasses.

"You know, this is completely fucking nuts," he said, turning back and testing the rope around his shoulders. Obeying Yamamoto-san's directions, Ben lay down on the surface of the boulder overlooking the valley below. The rope slowly played out as Ben sank further head-first over the rock's edge. Then with a hand around Ben's legs, our guide made one final push and dangled him over the brink. Only Ben's sneakered feet were visible. A burst of wind swept up from the trees below.

"Shit!" I heard Ben's shriek echo.

"Do you promise to be a good teacher and treat your students fairly?" Yamamoto-san bellowed into the wind.

"*Hai!*"

"Do you promise to be a good and faithful husband to your wife?"

"*Hai!*"

"Do you promise to be a good and loving father to your children?"

"*HAI!*"

I grabbed the rope more tightly as I felt myself slipping forward, bracing my feet against whatever roots and rocks I could.

"Do you promise to obey the laws of gods and nature and to be an upright human being?"

"*HAI!* Oh, GOD, *HAI! HAI!*"

Yamamoto-san reached down and grabbed the rope. I yanked as hard as I could, and we pulled Ben back into the land of the living.

He was sweating, shaking and pale, but bowed to Yamamoto-san, saying without a trace of sarcasm, "Thank you, Yamamoto-san. Thank you very much."

He turned to me wide-eyed, the rope still wrapped around him. "Matt, I just saw my life flash before me.

Literally. I swear, I have never been more frightened in my fucking life."

Yamamoto-san chose that moment to smile at us.

"Well done," he said. "You are now reborn. You, too?"

Me? I hesitated. I knew that it was an honor. Outsiders in the country, outsiders to the religion. Ben and I weren't a part of the tradition, and yet had been given even the smallest glimpse of what lay beyond.

But I wasn't ready to be reborn. I shook my head and declined the offer with a bow of my own. "Not today," I apologized. "I'm not ready."

He nodded and waved to us. "Go down the back path, to Dorogawa. That way takes you to O-miné and home."

We said thank you and bowed again, then followed the path he indicated. After a few moments, we lost sight of him, and then paused to ask ourselves. Hadn't we already been on O-miné?

As we reached the temple, we realized that Yamamoto-san had been right. The temple itself was O-miné. A nearby map sign told us that the mountain was called Mt. Sanjyo-Gatake, and only the temple was O-miné. The rock cliff was Nishi no Nozoki: The View of the West.

"Do you want to go to O-miné?" I asked Ben, as he crossed his arms and looked at the lone blue-tiled covered wooden structure. About a dozen older Japanese men in polo shirts, small white towels draped over their necks, were milling about the vacant dirt lot in front of the building. A few were taking photos while others were texting on their mobile phones.

"Nah," he said finally, hiking up his backpack straps with his left hand. "I saw what I came to see."

And we turned and began our descent to the village below.

## About the Author

Originally from Troy, New York, M. Thomas Apple spent part of his childhood in a tiny hamlet in the Helderbergs and his teenage years in a slightly larger village in the Adirondacks. He studied languages and literature as an undergraduate student at Bard College and later creative writing at the University of Notre Dame du Lac, where he wrote a controversial, award-winning weekly column for the student-run daily newspaper, *The Observer*.

After further studies in education at Temple University, he now teaches global issues and English as a second language at Ritsumeikan University in Kyoto, Japan. He lives in a house co-designed with his wife and partially decorated by his two daughters, nestled in the foothills of the mountains and surrounded by lots and lots of Japanese cedar and cicada.